An Hour in the Morning

An Hour in the Morning

by
GORDON COOPER

illustrated by
Philip Gough

E. P. DUTTON & CO., INC.   NEW YORK

First published in the U.S.A. 1974 by E. P. Dutton & Co.

Copyright © 1971 by Gordon Cooper

LIBRARY OF CONGRESS CATALOGING IN PUBLICATION DATA

Cooper, Gordon.   An hour in the morning.

SUMMARY: A twelve-year-old girl passes her labour
examination and becomes a general maid to a well-to-do
farm family in early twentieth-century England.

[1. England—Social life and customs—Fiction]
I. Gough, Philip, illus.   II. Title.

PZ7.C7853Ho3   [Fic]   73-19671   ISBN 0-525-32295-7

Printed in the U.S.A.   First Edition

for
EMMA COOPER

Chapter 1

Miss Crompton looked at her watch. It was ten minutes to four. School would soon be over. She glanced round the room at the forty children sitting in five rows, her sharp eyes searching for any signs of inattention among the boys who were wearing brown corduroy suits and the girls who were dressed in blouses and skirts and long, white pinafores. They all appeared to be listening to the story which was being read to them.

The school had been built in 1854, and even now, after sixty years had passed, very little had changed. The classroom was long and narrow, and was heated by a small iron stove surrounded by a fireguard. There were three windows, but they were set high so that no one could day-dream by looking out of them. There were no pictures on the walls. The only form of decoration was a large map of the world, with all the parts of the British Empire coloured pink. England itself was only a small country, yet it had many links with the rest of the world, and there were many areas of pink, both large and small, on the map. Apart from Miss Crompton's desk set on a low platform, the only other furniture was a tall cupboard where the few books and slates were kept. Miss Crompton would have liked to have had more books, but there was not a great deal of money to be spent in a village school, and the school funds were administered by the vicar, who expected a long explanation of why any purchases should be made. The book from which Kate Bassett was reading aloud to the class was one of Miss Crompton's own, one which she had been given a long time ago when she was a girl. She stood at the back of the classroom and watched Kate Bassett as she read. She was twelve years old, a tall girl with a fresh complexion and brown hair drawn back from her face and tied with a black ribbon. In her brown blouse and skirt, long white pinafore, and black boots she appeared to be no different from the other girls in the class. But she is different, thought Miss Crompton. If only there were more like her, trying to teach forty children whose ages ranged from five to thirteen would not seem such an impossible task. It was Friday afternoon, and at quarter past four Miss Crompton would make her weekly visit to the vicarage, where she would discuss the work of the school for the coming week with the vicar. Today she would also tell him of the plan which had been forming in her mind for several weeks. The plan was for Kate Bassett.

'I think we must end there,' she said, her harsh voice cutting across Kate's softer tones. 'It's time to go home. Thank you, Kate.'

She waited until Kate had returned to her seat, and then she walked to the front of the classroom and stood by her desk.

'Everyone stand,' she said, and waited with pursed lips for the noise of the clatter of heavy boots on scrubbed floorboards to subside, and then she read the home-going prayer. Another week was over.

'School dismissed,' said Miss Crompton, and she stood by the door as the children went out into the cloakroom.

'And no talking,' she said angrily, as they rushed to the row of pegs to find their caps, hats, and coats. The boys ran off, glad to be free of school for two whole days, and there was room in the narrow passage for elder sisters to help the smaller children with buttons and hair ribbons and to collect the rush baskets in which they had brought their midday meal to school.

After they had gone, Miss Crompton put on her own coat and hat and walked to the vicarage for her weekly meeting with the vicar. In his study they discussed the attendance figures, the amount of chalk used, the number of slates broken, and the names of the children who were to be prepared for confirmation. Miss Crompton thought that the vicar seemed rather preoccupied. He did not ask how it was that five slates had been broken, so she was spared the embarrassment of telling him that she had knocked them off her desk with her own elbow when she had jumped up to rap a boy on the head with her thimble. She did not know that the vicar had received a letter from his son's tutor at Oxford complaining of the young man's poor attendance at university lectures. The vicar wanted the meeting with Miss Crompton to end as quickly as possible so that he could continue the long letter he was writing to his son.

'Well, everything seems satisfactory, Miss Crompton,' he said. 'Now, if there is nothing else?'

'There is the matter of Kate Bassett,' said Miss Crompton firmly.

'Oh yes,' said the vicar. 'You wish me to make the arrangements for her to sit the Labour Examination.'

'No,' said Miss Crompton, her pale face colouring with a certain eagerness as she began the speech which she had already rehearsed several times at home in front of the mirror in her sitting-room. 'In the ten years that I have taught at Bretherton school I think she is the best pupil I have ever had.'

'I am sure that she is a credit to your methods,' said the vicar, kindly.

'I had thought,' said Miss Crompton firmly, 'that she might be encouraged to remain at school with the idea of becoming a pupil-teacher.'

The vicar looked at her in surprise.

'I see,' he said slowly. 'You realize that we have never had a pupil-teacher at the school before?'

'Yes,' said Miss Crompton, 'but Kate Bassett is an exceptional girl. She will have no difficulty in passing the Labour Examination. Then it will be too late. She would be able to leave school at Easter.'

'Would that be such a bad thing?' asked the vicar. 'I believe that there are several children in the family. One less at home would make all the difference.'

'I have never had much respect for the ideas behind the Labour Examination,' replied Miss Crompton. 'It is as if education is something to be got through as quickly as possible. If Kate Bassett was a dull girl, she would have to drag on at school until she was fourteen. Because she is clever and will be able to pass examinations, she can leave when she is twelve.'

'I think that you must surely be aware that these are hard times, Miss Crompton, and we must face the facts as they are,' said the vicar. 'If Kate Bassett remained at school it would be several years before she could earn any money. In all that time she would be dependent upon her father for her clothing and for her keep. Wages are not very high in this part of the country, and life is difficult for the people in the cottages.'

'I know,' said Miss Crompton, thinking of the worn-out boots and the patched pinafores of her pupils, and the amount of food brought in the rush baskets to be eaten at midday. Some of the older boys ate the slices of bread and butter, or bread and lard, at ten o'clock, and then had nothing else until they went home for tea.

'Have you spoken to the girl of your interest in her?' went on the vicar.

'No, sir,' said Miss Crompton. 'I realized that I must speak to you first.'

'I think you have been very wise,' said the vicar, leaning back in his chair. 'It is no good upsetting the girl with high-flown plans which would only leave her discontented when she found that they could come to nothing. Her parents wouldn't thank you for it. I think it best that I write to the school at Chaxton and arrange for her to sit the examination. Now, is there anything else?'

'No,' said Miss Crompton. 'Good afternoon, sir.'

She curtsied slowly and walked back to the schoolhouse. She lived alone and there was no one to whom she could confide her hopes and disappointments. She had tried to do for Kate Bassett the same thing that a teacher had done for her, Alice Crompton, twenty-five years ago. She had been living at Chaxton, going to the church school near the cathedral close. A teacher there, Miss Huntley, had helped her. She had gone to her home and spoken to her parents, explaining that with her intelligence and ability, Alice could become a teacher. She was their only child and Mr. and Mrs. Crompton had agreed that she should have her chance. She thought back over the years to the time when she was a pupil-teacher and then of the years that she had spent in a school at Bath. When her father had died, she came back to Chaxton to live with her mother, teaching at the same school where she herself had once been a pupil. Ten years later her mother died, and then she had come to the school at Bretherton. She was not an inspired teacher as Miss Huntley had been. Even allowing for the narrow syllabus she was required to teach, she was unable to give the children an awareness of the world in which they lived. In later years there had been the problems of class discipline, and she had come to rely upon a sharp tongue, a thimble, and a cane. She had never really enjoyed her work, until she became aware of Kate Bassett. Miss Crompton allowed herself no favourites among her pupils but she had hoped to save her if she possibly could from the small future which would be hers, but she had failed. And there is nothing I can do to help her, thought Miss Crompton, sadly.

At the vicarage, the vicar finished the letter he was writing to his son. He reminded him of the sacrifices that had been made to enable him to study at Oxford. 'I only ask,' he wrote, 'that your talents be used to the full. I think that one of the greatest sins of all is that of waste—waste of talent and waste of opportunity.'

He sealed the envelope, pleased with what he had written, and then he took up his pen again and wrote to the school authorities in Chaxton, to make arrangements for Kate Bassett to take the Labour Examination.

Kate Bassett walked home from school carrying her sister Rose on her back, unaware that her future was being decided.

A few days later Maggie Leeves, the kitchen-maid at the vicarage, brought a note to the schoolhouse door. It was from Mr. Willis, the vicar, informing Miss Crompton that the arrangements had been made for Kate to go to Chaxton on the last Monday in the month.

On the afternoon of the Sunday before the examination Aunt Em, Mr. Bassett's sister, paid her fortnightly visit to her brother's house. With her gleaming black hair strained back into a bun and her full red cheeks, she always reminded Kate of a wooden Dutch doll that she had been given one Christmas and which had been handed down to all the Bassett girls in turn and was now the property of May, with whom it was a firm favourite. Kate was the eldest. Then there was Mary who was ten, eight-year-old Teddy, Rose aged six, and the twins Jimmy and May who were four.

'It's easy to remember how old our Kate is,' Mrs. Bassett used to say. 'She was born exactly a year after Queen Victoria died.'

Aunt Em always considered that she was a generous-minded woman, and whenever she visited the small cottage on the outskirts of the village she always brought something for Mrs. Bassett from her store cupboard. This time it was a jar of blackberry jelly which looked as if it was not keeping very well. Aunt Em was a thrifty housekeeper. Her store cupboard was like a shop, with row upon row of pots and jars all neatly labelled on the shelves.

'If I didn't pick another blackberry for five years your Uncle Percy could still have a blackberry tart every Sunday,' she would say, but when the blackberries were ripe she would be out in the woods with an old milking pail, picking the fruit as fast as she was able. It never occurred to her that perhaps her husband would have liked a different pudding on an occasional Sunday.

Uncle Percy, Aunt Em's husband, was one of the gamekeepers at Ellswood Park, which was a very beautiful Elizabethan manor house surrounded by many acres of woods and parklands. There were four carriage drives to the estate and Uncle Percy and Aunt Em lived in the lodge at the southern entrance. Aunt Em was deeply conscious of her position as a gamekeeper's wife. She felt set apart from the rest of the people of Bretherton. 'Working for gentry,' she would say, 'makes a person just that bit different.' She felt quite sure that no one could open the lodge gates so swiftly as she could, and no curtsy was so respectful or graceful as hers as Lady Margaret Carey's carriage passed by. South Lodge was a much larger house than the Bassetts' cottage, but to Aunt Em's annoyance, her brother and his wife always seemed happy there, even if the rooms were small and dark.

'I'd make a few changes if ever I had to live there,' Aunt Em often said to Uncle Percy. 'Not that my advice would ever be asked for.' She and Uncle Percy had no children, but that did not prevent her from giving advice to her brother's wife on the subject of bringing up a family. Aunt Em thought that if you were pretty it stood to reason that you didn't have much sense, and so she was quite ready to give Mrs. Bassett her views on any subject, from the making of rugs to the cutting out of blouses. She liked bright colours, and this particular Sunday afternoon she sat at the parlour window, resplendent in her new purple costume.

'The children are just turning the corner of the lane,' she announced. 'And not before time, either. You'd think that they'd know better than to be loitering about the village on a Sunday afternoon.'

'There's a new circuit minister at the chapel,' said Mrs. Bassett. 'He's known for his long sermons.'

'Oh,' said Aunt Em in a disappointed tone. 'I can never keep up with all the changes at Green Lane Chapel. Mr. Willis at the vicarage has been at the church for nearly twenty years.' She turned again to the window. 'Your Kate is getting to be a big girl,' she said, glancing at her brother, sitting in his tall, high-backed chair. 'I should have thought that it was time that her feet were under someone else's table.'

'They can't be children for very long,' said Mr. Bassett. 'If she passes that exam tomorrow, she'll leave school at Easter.'

'Do you think she will pass?' said Aunt Em, doubtfully.

'Miss Crompton seemed to think so,' said Mrs. Bassett.

'She must take after our side of the family,' replied Aunt Em. 'I was always reckoned to be a scholar when I was at school.'

She was too busy watching the children from the window to see the amused glance which passed between Mr. and Mrs. Bassett.

'Handsome is as handsome does,' she went on. 'Still, if she does leave school at Easter, she'd better be looking for a place. I could ask Mrs. Bingham at Ellswood Park if she'll be wanting a scullery-maid. It would be as good a place as any to start. If Kate looked after herself she might work up to be a parlour-maid. Gentry usually like their girls tall. Mind you, I'd have to speak early. Girls come from miles around to get work at the Park.'

'I think that it would be a hard place for a young girl,' Mrs. Bassett said. 'Lady Margaret does so much entertaining. There are all those dinner parties she gives.'

'Well, I'm sure that no one knows that better than I do,' said

Aunt Em, stiffly. 'Haven't I those lodge gates to see to? Sometimes there's as many as eight carriages in as many minutes. No sooner have I sat myself down, then I have to get up and open the gates again.'

'We'll see when the time comes,' said Mrs. Bassett in the quiet but firm tone in which she often spoke to Aunt Em.

'Well, I'm sure that you know best,' Aunt Em said in a voice that showed quite clearly that she thought otherwise. 'I only thought that I would be doing the girl a good turn, that's all.'

She turned again to the window and watched the children as they came up the garden path. Teddy was in front, then came Mary and Rose, and last of all Kate, with Jimmy and May on either side of her. Aunt Em again thought how tall Kate was getting. The brown coat that she was wearing seemed rather tight under the arms and short in the sleeves. As far as I can see, thought Aunt Em, it will be a good thing if she can leave school at Easter. A new coat and a pair of boots wouldn't come amiss. It's time that she was out earning.

Perhaps it was more fortunate than Kate realized that Aunt Em was broadly built and not very tall, otherwise after two or three years had passed she might have received the gift of a purple costume.

Aunt Em turned from the window as the younger children came into the parlour. The twins hung back when they saw her. She was not a very welcoming person.

'Haven't you got a kiss for your poor old auntie, then?' said Aunt Em, and she allowed herself to be kissed by Teddy and Rose and Jimmy and May. The children did not stay by her side, but sat on the floor near their father's chair. They did not see him much during the week as he was up early in the morning and came home late. It was always something of a treat to have him at home. Mr. Bassett was the shepherd for Mr. Blake at Glebe Farm, and during the lambing season he would be away for several days at a time, living alone in his shepherd's hut. Sometimes he would bring home the very frail lambs to be cared for by Mrs. Bassett in the kitchen until they were strong enough to go back to the fold. It was hard to realize that he and Aunt Em were brother and sister. His calm strength of manner contrasted so oddly with Aunt Em's sharp, angry ways.

Aunt Em looked up when Mary and Kate came in from the

passage where they had been hanging up the hats and coats. Although she was Aunt Em's favourite, Mary was a little afraid of her, but she came over and dutifully kissed her red cheek. 'There's a good girl,' said Aunt Em warmly, gazing at her fondly. 'And how are you, Kate?' she went on in her usual sharp manner.

'Very well, thank you, Aunt Em,' said Kate, thinking how much nicer the Sunday afternoons were when Aunt Em was not there.

'Tall as ever, I see,' said Aunt Em. 'I should think that you must be the biggest girl in the school.'

Kate always felt uncomfortable when Aunt Em came to visit. She knew that she was tall for her age, but nothing, not even Aunt Em, could make her stop growing. She felt the colour rise in her cheeks.

'You've no call to go reddening up like that,' said Aunt Em. 'Perhaps it will be just as well if you do manage to pass this examination I've been hearing about. Then you'll be able to get out into the world. That will soon knock the corners off you.'

'Will you come and help me with the tea, Kate, please?' said Mrs. Bassett with a smile, and Kate followed her out into the kitchen, feeling that she would rather cut a whole mountain of bread and butter than have to stay in the parlour with Aunt Em.

In bed that evening she lay awake, thinking about the examination she would take at Chaxton the next day. 'I don't think that you will have very much to worry about,' Miss Crompton had said. 'Just write as clearly as you can, and don't try to work too quickly.' The vicar had wished her luck, telling her that it would be a great honour for the school and what a fine thing it would be for her parents if she was able to pass the examination and leave school and go out to work. Kate was not really sure that she wanted to leave school. During the last three months, instead of doing needlework which she hated, Miss Crompton had allowed her to help the younger children in the school with learning the alphabet and the multiplication tables. She had even taken off her silver watch and allowed Kate to hold it close to the children's ears so that they might know the sound the letter 't' made. At home Kate had always helped her mother with her brothers and sisters, and she found that she looked forward to the two afternoons each week when the sewing bags were handed out by Lily Smith and Jessie Banks, and instead of having to hem dusters and tea towels, Miss Crompton would tell her to sit with the five- and six-year-olds in the front of the classroom and help them with their lessons. Sometimes Miss Crompton told her to use the blackboard, and gave her a small encouraging smile on the first few occasions, even when the chalk kept on breaking and the time when she almost knocked the blackboard off its easel. She remembered the time when Tommy Hawkins, who for some unknown reason had been unable to write the letters 's' and 'f', suddenly filled his slate with three rows of each, and she had felt a sense of delight and relief that he would no longer incur Miss Crompton's anger. She had never told her mother of what she did at school on Tuesday and Thursday afternoons. There was no need, because Mary and Teddy were immensely proud of what she did and always told Mrs. Bassett about the sewing afternoons.

Kate had often thought that it must be a wonderful thing to be a teacher. Miss Crompton had been able to read so many books and seemed to know everything that there was to know. Sometimes she thought of all the books there must be just waiting for people to read them. She did not know how one became a teacher. She could not ask her father or mother because they would not know, and Miss Crompton had never said anything to her when school ended on Tuesday and Thursday afternoons, but just watched her silently as she cleaned the blackboard and put the slates back on the third shelf of the cupboard.

At Bretherton, when it was time for them to leave school, if their fathers were tradesmen, the boys usually went to work with them at the bakery, the wheelwright's shop, or at the blacksmith's forge, but in most cases they were employed on the farms. Sometimes girls were apprenticed to dressmakers, but usually they went into domestic service, near at home at first, and then they moved away into the towns and cities as they grew older. Kate thought that this would probably happen to her. It was what both her mother and Aunt Em had done. Just before she went to sleep, she wondered what it would be like to live and work in someone else's house.

Chapter 2

The next morning Kate was driven into Chaxton by Mr. Pearce, the carter from Glebe Farm. It was the first time that she had ever left the village of Bretherton, and everything she saw on the way was new and exciting. Mr. Pearce had made the same journey to the mill at Chaxton every week for at least ten years, but Kate's great interest in everything made him feel that he was seeing the familiar landscape for the first time too.

They saw a herd of red deer in Sir John Baxter's park, and the carter showed her the house in which his mother and father had lived when they were first married and where he himself had been born. On the downs there was a place where the turf had been cut away in the shape of a cross to commemorate a battle that had been fought in Anglo-Saxon times. When they left the lanes and came on to the main road they began to see other carts going in the direction of Chaxton, and Kate felt a thrill of excitement when Mr. Pearce said that when they turned the next corner they would be able to see the spire of the cathedral. She gave a little gasp of pleasure when she saw it. The spire seemed to soar into the sky, almost as if it were floating on air, but it seemed so slender and delicate that you would have wondered how it had withstood rain and rough winds for more than seven hundred years.

'What's that place, Mr. Pearce?' Kate asked, as they passed a long drive leading to a big, grey, square building.

'That's the workhouse, maid,' said Mr. Pearce. 'Let's hope we never see the inside of those walls.'

Kate thought of Mrs. Lewis and her three children. When Mr. Lewis had died, the cottage in which they lived had been needed for the new man who had taken his place as a farmhand at Ellswood Park, and Mrs. Lewis and Winnie, Tom, and Lily had to go and live in the workhouse. She wondered what it must be like having no home of your own, and having to live somewhere behind those grey, sad-looking walls.

'There's the wharf, maid,' said Mr. Pearce, and Kate saw the big, black barges piled high with coal and tiles, floating on the canal.

'If you had a ride on one of them,' he said, 'you could go all the way to London.'

When they came into the main street, Mr. Pearce appeared to be a well-known figure. Several people called out in greeting, and Kate, perched up on the front of the waggon behind the big grey carthorse, smiled back at them.

'Yon's the school,' said Mr. Pearce, pointing to a red-bricked building with a railed-in playground. 'I'll be leaving the mill at about twelve. Mind you're here, then, maid.'

'Thank you, Mr. Pearce,' said Kate, as she jumped down from the waggon. Compared with the school at Bretherton, the Chaxton school loomed very large. A girl of Kate's own age with auburn hair was waiting at the gate.

'Have you come for the examination?' she asked.

'Yes,' said Kate.

'Come with me, then,' said the girl. 'I'll show you where we have to go.'

The examination was being held in a room at the end of a long corridor. The girl, whose name was Nancy, told Kate that it was the room normally used by the older pupils, but for this morning they had to move in with another class. Nancy lived in Chaxton and attended this school.

'There are two of us taking the examination from here,' she said, 'and four boys and two girls are coming in from the villages.'

Nancy was the only candidate who appeared to be quite at ease and chatted away quite calmly, although the other boys and girls sat quietly and said very little. She stopped talking only when the head teacher came into the room with some papers in his hand. She was called upon to hand out pens, ink, and paper, which she did, raising her eyebrows and winking broadly at Kate. The teacher looked at a large pocket watch.

'Right,' he said. 'You may start now. Remember to write your name clearly on every piece of paper you use.'

Kate found that the arithmetic questions were not so very different from those which Miss Crompton gave her to do, and except for a long division sum which gave a remainder of thirteen, she felt quietly pleased when the time came for the papers to be handed in.

'Everyone is to go into the playground now,' said the teacher, 'and I don't want to hear any talking or shouting. Remember that for everyone else in the school, this is a normal working day, and lessons will be going on as usual.'

'Come on,' said Nancy, taking Kate's arm. 'I'll show you where to go. How did you get on?' she said, when they were out in the playground. 'Do you think that you'll pass?'

'I hope so,' said Kate. 'I don't know about that last sum, though.'

'I didn't get as far as that,' said Nancy with a sigh. 'But I would like to leave school and go out to work.'

'What will you do?' asked Kate.

'Well,' replied Nancy, 'my sister's in service at Doctor Crawford's house, and my mother wants me to do the same kind of work. She always says that it's the best thing for a girl, and that you can always tell somebody who's been in gentleman's service because they know the right way to do anything. You can earn a lot more money in the tobacco factory though, and at the end of the day at least you can come home. And you've got Sunday to yourself. What will you do, Kate?'

'I expect I'll go into service,' said Kate.

'There's not much to choose from, is there?' said Nancy with a rueful grin. 'And I suppose that it's even worse when you live in the country. What I'd really like to do is to work in a shop— somewhere like Billington's in the market-place. But even there you've got to live in, and they do say that the housekeeper there is a real old misery and keeps the girls short of food. Look out, here comes the gaffer!' she added quickly, and Kate turned and saw the headmaster coming towards them.

'We're ready for the reading examination now,' he said. 'You will come in alphabetical order. Kate Bassett . . .'

'Good luck,' called Nancy, as Kate hurried off behind the teacher, and was shown into a small room where the reading inspector was waiting.

'Let me see, Kate Bassett from the school at Bretherton, isn't it, and from the admirable Miss Crompton?' he said. 'Sit down at the desk, then.'

He smiled at her encouragingly as he gave her a large Bible and

13

asked her to read Psalm 121. At first Kate found that her hands were trembling and she could hardly turn the pages.

'Take your time,' said the inspector quietly. He was a small man with a lined face and grey hair.

'I will lift up mine eyes,' began Kate, and suddenly she was calm and began to read in a firm, pleasant voice. When she had finished, the inspector handed her a newspaper and asked her to read a paragraph, watching her intently as she read without any hesitation.

'Thank you, Kate,' said the inspector, looking at her quizzically. 'Do you think that you are ready for the big, wide world?'

'I don't know, sir,' said Kate.

'And it takes a whole lifetime to find out,' said the inspector, with a twinkle. 'That will be all, thank you.'

There was a soft light in his eyes as he watched Kate leave the room. His own daughter had once had the same quiet grace.

When Kate came out into the corridor, Nancy was awaiting her turn. She looked as if she would have liked to have said something, but the headmaster was there and she had to content herself with raising her eyebrows as high as they could go. The headmaster asked Kate if arrangements had been made for her to return to Bretherton and when she explained that Mr. Pearce would be calling at twelve o'clock, he suggested that she might like to look round the town. 'Mind that you don't get up to any mischief,' he added.

It gave Kate a delightful holiday feeling to be able to explore Chaxton. At Bretherton, only Lady Margaret's carriage and waggons from the farms were to be seen in the village street, but in Chaxton there was a great deal of activity. Carts went by carrying goods to and from the wharf, men pushed barrows containing fruit and vegetables, and the carriages driven by smartly liveried grooms all combined to create a busy atmosphere. In the wide streets and squares there were four-storied houses of mellowed stone with basement kitchens which were reached by flights of steps leading directly from the pavement. Anyone working there would look out at the iron railings protecting the area steps, and Kate thought that it must be like being in prison. She passed an old knife-grinder with his cart, and a maid in a pink print dress waited with a basket over her arm for her knives to be sharpened. The spire soared above all the other buildings of the town and Kate made her way to the close, where the clergy houses, set in high-walled gardens, faced across the green to the cathedral. Nurse-maids went by pushing high-wheeled perambulators and two old clergymen smiled at Kate from behind steel-rimmed spectacles. After the bustle of the streets, the close had an air of calm and quiet as serene as the great church itself.

Kate never forgot her first visit to the cathedral. As she pushed open the heavy oak door it seemed to her that the Norman arches supporting the carved roof emblazoned with coats of arms soared into t e air like fountains made of stone. She stood looking up the broad nave to the high altar which was draped with a rich purple brocade trimmed with red and white and she thought that never before had she seen anything so beautiful. On the walls there were memorial tablets bearing the names of people who had died many years ago, and she wondered what sort of people they had been and if the houses in which they had lived still stood in Chaxton. There was a lectern with the Bible resting on the outspread wings of an eagle which gleamed like gold in the soft light which came through the latticed windows. A flight of steps, carpeted in red, led to the pulpit which had figures of angels carved on its wooden canopy. In one of the side chapels there was a Tudor monument with a knight and his lady carved in marble lying side by side, their hands clasped in everlasting prayer as they faced the altar. Kate thought that the knight with his sharp-pointed beard wore a stern expression, but the lady's face above a wide-fluted ruff looked serene and kind. Someone was playing the organ and the great notes rang in triumph down the nave. She sat for a few minutes listening to the music and thought of the yellow varnished pews and whitewashed walls of the chapel in Green Lane and of the old harmonium with the noisy foot pedals which only old Mr. Blease could coax into tune.

As she came out again into the close the cathedral clock struck eleven and she made her way towards the market-place to see the shops. At the edge of the pavements there were the hitching rails where horses could be tethered while their owners did their shopping. The most important-looking building was the Corn Exchange where farmers met to transact their business and where all the auction sales were held. A flight of wide steps led up to two green doors with pillars on each side, and in between there was a statue of a woman holding a sheaf of corn and wearing a wreath of flowers in her hair. Carved at the foot of the statue was the name 'Ceres'. Kate thought that Billington's, the draper's shop that Nancy had spoken of, was very imposing. It had two windows, one of which was filled with household linen, sheets and blankets

16

and eiderdowns and table-cloths, and in the other there was a display of dress materials and trimmings. A man in a long, black tailed coat stood in the shop doorway and bowed to the customers as they went inside. At the fishmonger's a man with a big black moustache and wearing a straw hat was arranging fish on blocks of ice, while another was busy placing pheasants on long hooks. On the shelves of a baker's shop there were tarts and pastries and cottage loaves, which were really two loaves in one, made by placing a circle of dough on top of a larger one and baking them together, with the result that each loaf looked like a rather squat figure eight. Kate's mother had four brothers and three sisters and she had told Kate that when they were children they used to take turns in having the larger slices of bread from the bottom of the loaf. 'We used to call them top and bottom days,' she said with a smile.

At the milliner's shop a grey-haired woman was arranging hats and feather boas in the window. One hat was decorated with pink silk flowers and she smiled when she saw Kate looking at it with obvious admiration. When the cathedral clock struck again, she was surprised to find that it was half past eleven, and so she walked back towards the school to wait for Mr. Pearce. She hoped that she might see Nancy again, but no one was in sight, and Kate thought that after the excitement of the examination the school had settled down to its usual routine of lessons. Soon after twelve, Mr. Pearce came by with the waggon.

'How did you get on, then, maid?' he asked, as Kate climbed up beside him.

'I don't know,' said Kate, happily, 'but I've had a lovely morning.'

Miss Crompton asked her the same question when she went back to the school and made her write a composition entitled 'My Visit to Chaxton'. When the teacher read the four closely written pages, she thought sadly that the writer would soon be gone from the school for ever. On the Friday of the following week the vicar came to the school, smiling broadly with a letter in his hand. She knew what he had come to say, and for her there was no pleasure in the news that Kate had passed the examination and could leave school at the end of the term. When the vicar announced the news to the school, she bowed stiffly when he reminded the children that it was due to the excellence of Miss

17

Crompton's teaching methods that Kate Bassett had done so well.

For Kate there was the thrill of achievement, mingling with the thought that her childhood must soon end. After Easter she would no longer have to walk the three miles to the school. Every morning the Bassett children set out early, with Rose and Teddy in front and Mary and Kate behind, with Kate carrying the children's dinners in the small rush basket. Sometimes they were given a ride on a passing farm cart, but usually they had to walk. Very often Rose was tired, and Mary took the basket while Rose was carried on Kate's back. The school bell would be ringing as they passed the church and they would have to run the last few yards into the playground, where Miss Crompton would be waiting with her cane and steel thimble. The school was close to the church and Mr. Willis, the vicar, who was one of the school governors, came to give the children scripture lessons. The other governor was Lady Margaret Carey from Ellswood Park and every Wednesday morning one of the grooms drove her to the school in a smart green and black pony trap. The first time that Kate had ever seen her she thought that it must be Queen Alexandra who stood in the doorway of the classroom because Miss Crompton curtsied right down to the floor and all the children jumped up from their seats with a great clatter of slates and heavy boots. Kate had been five years old and it was her first week at the school, yet she could still remember the beautiful high pearl collar and pendant ear-rings Lady Margaret had worn. Most of the houses in Bretherton formed part of the Ellswood Park estate, and she was almost a legendary figure. Although Miss Crompton would have already called the register at nine o'clock before lessons began, Lady Margaret would sit at her desk and call the register all over again. Sometimes she pronounced the children's names incorrectly, which made them want to laugh, but they knew that Miss Crompton was there with her thimble and cane, watching them. Usually each child said, 'Yes, your ladyship,' when his or her name was called, but sometimes a dreamer would forget and say, 'Yes, Miss Crompton,' and Lady Margaret would repeat the name of the offender in a cold voice, while Miss Crompton moved purposefully down the classroom, her thimble finger raised.

On the day the children broke up for the Easter holidays Miss Crompton allowed school to end a quarter of an hour earlier. She stood at the door as the children filed out into the cloakroom. Kate was the last to leave.

'This is good-bye, then, Kate Bassett,' said Miss Crompton in a voice which seemed to be even more harsh than it usually was. 'I shall miss you on Tuesday and Thursday afternoons—and I expect the little ones will.'

I'm going to miss them too, thought Kate, and you, Miss Crompton.

'Good luck, Kate,' said Miss Crompton.

'Thank you, miss,' Kate replied, aware that the teacher was looking at her intently, and she realized with surprise that Miss Crompton was really rather pretty when she was not frowning and when her lips were not drawn into a thin, hard line.

'Off you go, then,' said Miss Crompton.

'Yes, miss,' said Kate. 'Good-bye.'

She went slowly out into the cloakroom, thinking sadly that she did not really want to leave school and go into service. She would have liked to have been able to come back after the holidays. Perhaps if there had been time enough, Miss Crompton might have been able to show her how to become a real teacher. But because she had passed the Labour Examination, her school-days were at an end.

'Come on, Kate!' called Mary, who was buttoning Rose's coat, and so she smiled and hurried forward and joined the other children in the noisy scramble for coats and dinner baskets.

'Race you to the gate,' said Mary.

'Right!' said Kate, seizing Rose's hand.

Miss Crompton watched the Bassett children as they ran across the playground, and then with a sigh she went back to her desk and crossed Kate's name from the school register.

Mr. and Mrs. Bassett had discussed Kate's future when the children were all in bed. Even if she had liked sewing, there was no money for her to be apprenticed to a dressmaker, and so she would enter domestic service. Aunt Em again suggested that she should speak to Mrs. Bingham at Ellswood Park, but from her own experience Mrs. Bassett knew that the life of a scullery- or kitchen-maid in a big house was not always a happy one. She also thought that Kate, at twelve years old, was too young to be a member of a staff as large as that of Ellswood Park.

'There's another thing,' said Aunt Em accusingly, 'and that's

19

your being chapel. Most of the gentry belong to the church and they expect their girls to be the same. You never find real gentry worshipping in a chapel. There might be a farmer or two, but never real gentry.'

It seemed to her that Mrs. Bassett was in no hurry to find Kate a situation.

'I should think,' she said to Uncle Percy, 'that my brother must be the talk of Bretherton—keeping a great girl like that at home, sitting around all day with nothing to do. She ought to be out making her way in the world instead of hanging about at home, being a burden to her parents.'

Kate was certainly not a burden to her parents. Mrs. Bassett found her a great help. Although the grey-stone tiled cottage in which the Bassetts lived was not very large, there were stone floors to be scrubbed and doorsteps to be whitened. There was water to be drawn from the well, washing and ironing to be done, Jimmy and May to be watched over, and food to be prepared for the chickens and pigs at the end of the garden, and Kate was kept quite busy enough for even Aunt Em to have been satisfied. After two weeks had passed, Mrs. Blake, the wife of the farmer for whom Mr. Bassett worked, wrote to some friends at Penrose Farm four miles away, telling them about Kate, and one afternoon a young lady drove up to the cottage to speak to Mrs. Bassett. Kate did not see her arrive because she was in the back garden, sitting on the old swing with May on her lap. Jimmy and May were pleased to have Kate at home all day because she could always be relied upon to invent new games for them to play. Then Mrs. Bassett came out to say that the lady had come to offer her work as a general maid, and Kate followed her into the parlour.

'This is Kate, Miss Linden,' said her mother, and a young woman rose from the chair in which only Mr. Bassett ever sat and held out her hand.

'How do you do, Kate?' she said, as Kate curtsied. 'I believe that you are looking for a situation, and as it happens I am looking for someone to help me because my sister is to be married in July.' She smiled. 'Your mother and I have been discussing terms. Your wages would be three shillings a week and you would come home on Sunday afternoons.'

Kate glanced at her mother, who nodded encouragingly.

'Well,' said Miss Linden. 'Would you like to come and live at
Penrose Farm?'

'Yes, please,' said Kate, looking at the tall figure in the dark
brown costume and white, high-necked blouse. There was something about Miss Linden's quiet, direct manner that she liked and

trusted. Three shillings a week seemed to Kate to be a large sum of money, and she thought how nice it must be to have money to spend.

'I should like you to start at the beginning of the month,' went on Miss Linden. 'Will that be all right, Mrs. Bassett?'

'Yes,' replied Kate's mother.

Kate stayed in the parlour watching Miss Linden and her mother walk down to the garden gate. They stood talking for a few minutes, and then Miss Linden drove away in a black pony trap with bright yellow wheels. Mrs. Bassett was smiling when she came back into the house. Kate was still really only a schoolgirl, and as her mother she was naturally anxious that she should be happy in her first time away from home. She had been impressed by Miss Linden's simple direct manner and she hoped that Kate would do well at Penrose Farm.

'Well, Kate?' said her mother.

Kate said nothing, but gave her a hug. She found the prospect of going away both exciting and frightening.

Chapter 3

There were just three weeks in which to get her clothes ready. Mrs. Bassett sat up late at night to make three blue print dresses and Kate tacked and hemmed and made caps and aprons. At South Lodge, Aunt Em said to Uncle Percy that she supposed she ought to help with Kate's clothes. After fifteen years of life with Aunt Em, Uncle Percy knew that when his wife supposed that she ought to do something, she had already decided that she would, and so he readily agreed.

'In that case,' said Aunt Em swiftly, 'I shall need some more money at the end of the week. I can't be expected to provide dresses out of the housekeeping. With prices what they are, it's as much as I can do to make the money go round as it is.'

This was not true. Right from the beginning of her married life Aunt Em had managed to save something each week from the housekeeping money. Upstairs on the landing at the bottom of an oak chest in which she kept her blankets there was a post office savings book which Uncle Percy did not know existed. He would have been surprised if he could have seen the figures recorded there. Every week Aunt Em went into Chaxton by carrier and paid some money into her post office account. If anyone from Bretherton was there, Aunt Em would wait until they had been served before she opened her handbag. At the end of the week when Uncle Percy asked her how much money she needed, she calculated the cost of two black afternoon dresses and added on half a crown. Uncle Percy gave her the extra money without asking any questions. As long as he had three good meals each day and two ounces of tobacco a week, he did not mind how Aunt Em spent the money he gave her. The dresses were made by a friend of Aunt Em's who was good with her needle, and who had once said to her that if ever there were any small dressmaking jobs which needed doing, she would be only too happy to oblige. When the dresses were finished, Aunt Em brought them to the cottage and made Kate try them on.

'Very handsome,' she said, 'or they will be when you've put your hair up and it's not hanging down your back in that untidy way.' She waved aside Kate's thanks.

'That's all right,' she said. 'Don't think that you've got to be beholden to me for the clothes on your back. I didn't want my brother's daughter to disgrace herself by not having anything decent to wear, that's all. Not that the Lindens are what I call real gentry. Not like they are up at Ellswood Park. Farmer Linden works alongside his men, and he only rents Penrose Farm. It actually belongs to the Careys. Still, they're comfortable enough, I dare say. One of the daughters is getting married, you said. I found out that it's the younger one. The other one will have to look sharp or else she'll be an old maid.'

On the last Sunday Kate packed all her possessions into the brown tin trunk which her father had bought for her, and her mother helped her to put up her hair.

'Don't strain it back too severely,' she said, showing Kate how to use the hairpins so that they did not hurt her head.

'You do look grown-up,' said Mary, who had watched all the activity surrounding Kate's departure with pride and interest. Kate certainly didn't feel grown-up. In chapel that afternoon she felt that everyone must be staring at her with her hair in a bun at the nape of her neck. The familiar hymns made her feel sad. At tea-time her throat felt so full that she could not eat the slice of fruit cake her mother had made as a special treat. Mrs. Bassett glanced at her, but said nothing. Kate was doing what she herself had done a long time ago, and she could still recall how she had felt. There was the feeling of excitement mingled with a sense of sadness. Mr. Bassett carried the brown tin trunk down the narrow stairs and tied it on to a small handcart while Kate put on her coat and hat. Her brothers and sisters gathered round her and May began to cry.

'Cheer up,' said Kate. 'I'll see you all in chapel next Sunday. I'm not going away for ever,' she added, with a little quiver in her voice.

'Of course not,' said her mother, 'and Sunday will soon come round again.'

They all came out to the gate to see Kate and Mr. Bassett set off.

When they reached the curve in the lane, Kate looked back at the old grey cottage with its low roof and small windows. The children had gone inside, but Mrs. Bassett was still standing there in her dark green blouse and grey skirt, and Kate suddenly realized that she had never seen her mother wearing a dress, but only skirts and blouses.

It was four miles to Penrose Farm, and despite her growing uneasiness, she felt a certain relief when her father said, 'This is it then, lass,' and she saw for the first time the dark red-bricked walls of her new home. The house had been built in Queen Anne's reign, and its three storeys had a warm, comfortable air. The garden was surrounded by a high wall, and as they passed the front gates of wrought iron she could see lawns and flower beds with a gravel path leading to an old oak door. Kate and her father walked down the lane at the side of the house until they came to a gate set in the garden wall. When they went inside, Miss Linden was waiting by the back door.

'Good evening, Mr. Bassett,' she said with a smile. 'Good evening, Kate. Welcome to Penrose Farm.'

She led the way up two flights of stairs, with Mr. Bassett following with the trunk, and Kate came last of all.

'This will be your room, Kate,' Miss Linden said, opening a door. 'I hope you will be comfortable here.' She smiled sympathetically. 'You can say good-bye to your father here and then come down when you are ready.'

'Oh, Dad,' said Kate, after Miss Linden had left them, and she put her face against the rough cloth of Mr. Bassett's coat.

'Now then, lass,' he said, 'you'll be all right once you've settled down.'

'Yes,' said Kate, after a little while.

'I must be getting back,' said Mr. Bassett gently, and they went downstairs to where Miss Linden was waiting.

'Walk with your father to the gate,' she said.

Kate felt very forlorn as she watched her father walk away. She hoped that he would turn back and wave, and she was disappointed when he did not. Then Miss Linden was behind her, with her hand on her shoulder.

'Now then, Kate,' she said briskly, 'I'll show you over the house, so that things won't seem so strange in the morning.'

Kate followed her along several passages and Miss Linden

opened what seemed to her to be an amazing number of doors which led into various rooms and to Kate everything seemed to be a confusing blur of heavy dark furniture and polished wood. Afterwards she was able to remember that in the hall there was a marble-topped table and a tall long-case clock with paintings of the seasons in the four corners of its face. In the dining-room there was a glass case in which there were two bluebirds perched on a twig, and in the drawing-room there were velvet-covered arm-chairs and a china cabinet, and in the window by the white lace curtains there was a fern trailing over the side of a brightly polished brass urn down to the floor.

In the kitchen Miss Linden showed Kate how to make cocoa. At home she had either tea or milk to drink. She had never tasted cocoa before, and she found that she liked its rich chocolate taste. There was also bread and cheese, but Kate did not think that she could eat anything.

'I think that I had better explain,' said Miss Linden, 'that my father and sister also live here at Penrose Farm. If you will call my sister Miss Grace, and call me Miss Nell, we shall all know where we are. The men always call my father the Master, so you may as well do the same.'

When Kate had finished her cocoa, Miss Nell said, 'You can go and unpack now. I'll call you in the morning at six o'clock. Good night, Kate.'

In the attic Kate unpacked her trunk and laid a blue print dress and a cap and an apron on the chair by the bedside ready for the morning. The room was larger than the one which she and Mary shared at home. The floorboards were bare and scrubbed white, but by the bed there was a rug of red and grey loops of cloth. The curtains and bed quilt were pale blue. In one corner of the room there was a washstand with a pink jug and basin and soap dish resting on its marble top. A white towel hung from a brass rod on the back of the door. Kate placed her clothes in the wardrobe and put her brush and comb on a small dressing-table on which stood a clock, a candlestick, and a little vase of primroses. For a while she lay in bed thinking of her mother and feeling very home-sick, and then she was asleep.

It was a quarter past five when she awoke. She went to the window and looked out. At the back of the house there was a large lawn with flower beds, and beyond them, fruit trees and a vegetable garden which stretched right to the garden wall. A path through a field led to the farm buildings and she could see several figures going in through a gate in readiness for a new day's work. She came back to the washstand and washed her face and hands in cold water and then began to dress. It was exactly six o'clock when there was a loud knock on her door and Kate came out on to the landing in her blue print dress and white cap and apron to find Miss Nell waiting for her.

'Well done, Kate,' she said. 'An hour in the morning is worth two in the afternoon.'

Everything was so very quiet as she followed Miss Nell down the back stairs and Kate wished that her new boots were not so squeaky. She saw that Miss Nell was wearing soft, dark slippers.

In the kitchen Miss Nell began to build up the fire in the kitchen range, carrying coal and wood from two large wooden boxes.

'On a farm we always need plenty of hot water,' she said, 'and I never let the fire in the range go out at all. Now, will you fill the two black kettles with water from the pump?'

Kate thought how different it was at home, where all the water had to be drawn from the well at the end of the garden. Sometimes in the summer months the well dried up, and then she and Mrs. Bassett would have to fetch water from a more fortunate neighbour, carrying it in buckets hanging from a wooden yoke which always made Kate's shoulder sore. She thought how Jimmy and May would have liked to have seen the water gushing out of the pump.

Next to the kitchen there was the scullery with a brick copper in the corner.

'We use the copper for the dairy work,' said Miss Nell. 'Will you fill it right to the brim, please?'

Kate had to fill a bucket nine times before the copper was full. She was careful not to spill any water on the dark red tiled floor.

'Do you think you can light the fire underneath?' asked Miss Nell. 'You know where we keep the wood and coal. You'll find a box of matches on the shelf.'

Kate laid the fire as she had seen her mother do in the kitchen at home, and whispered a fervent prayer that it would burn brightly. When she went back into the kitchen Miss Nell was filling two brass cans with hot water from the kettles on the range.

'These are for the Master and Miss Grace,' she explained. 'I cleaned a pair of the Master's boots last night. Will you fetch them from the scullery, Kate?'

They went upstairs, Miss Nell carrying the two cans of hot water and Kate carrying the pair of large brown boots which she had found in the scullery. Miss Nell stopped outside a green-painted door and placed one of the cans on the floor. She knocked and called, 'Are you awake, Father?'

A man's deep voice said, 'Righto, Nell,' and Miss Nell smiled and motioned to Kate to place the boots by the side of the hot water can. She set down the other brass can outside a cream-painted door and called, 'Are you awake, Grace?' and a light voice called back, 'All right, Nell.'

'Now, Kate,' said Miss Nell when they were back in the kitchen, 'while the Master and Miss Grace are getting up, I'm going to start getting the breakfast ready, and while I'm doing that I want you to clean the boots and shoes. You'll find everything you need in the scullery.'

There were two pairs of men's working boots, a best brown pair, two pairs of ladies' high laced black boots, and a pair of brown shoes. Kate thought that she must just see if the copper fire was burning, and she was relieved to see the leaping flames when she opened the little iron door under the copper. She spread a newspaper on the floor and began to clean the boots. She heard a man's voice speaking to Miss Nell, and then the sound of a door opening and closing. She looked out of the scullery door and saw a man walking down the garden path and out through the gate in the back of the garden wall. He was tall and broad-shouldered with grey hair. His arms seemed very brown against the blue and white of his striped shirt. Soon there were sounds of other movement in the house, and Kate heard a woman's voice and quick, light footsteps in the passage outside. Miss Nell was obviously still busy in the kitchen. The sharp scent of bacon frying crept under the door of the scullery, and Kate realized how hungry she was. When the boots and shoes were all cleaned, she set them out in a row. Her own boots were rather dusty from last night's walk, so she bent down and put some black polish on them. As she was shining them with a soft duster she was aware of Miss Nell standing in the doorway watching her, and she felt her face burn and redden, almost as if she had done something wrong.

'That's right,' said Miss Nell, looking at the row of boots and shoes with approval. 'Make yourself look smart. When you're ready, we'll go into the dairy.'

The dairy was a large room with a dark red tiled floor. A young woman in a green dress was pouring cream into a butter churn.

'This is Kate,' said Miss Nell, and the young woman looked up and smiled.

'I was out last night when you came,' she said, holding out her hand. 'I'm Miss Grace.'

She was slenderly built, with fair hair. As she curtsied, Kate felt big and clumsy beside her, but Miss Grace's manner was kind.

'I hope that you will be happy here with us,' she said.

She finished pouring the cream into the churn and showed Kate how to turn the handle. She and Miss Nell stood watching her for a few minutes and then they went back into the kitchen. Kate did not know how long it would take to churn the cream into butter, so she went on turning the handle of the churn until Miss Grace came back.

'I expect you're ready for your breakfast, Kate,' she said. 'Off you go now.'

Kate found that she was very hungry and she hurried into the kitchen, but stood rather shyly in the doorway when she saw that a man was there, drinking a cup of tea. She did not quite know what to do, but Miss Nell looked up and said, 'It's all right, Kate. Come along in. This is the Master.'

It was the same man whom Kate had seen walking down the garden path.

'So you're Kate,' he said.

'Yes, sir,' said Kate curtsying. Mr. Linden stood looking at her and Kate thought that his eyes were kind.

'Don't get working too hard on your first day,' he said with a smile.

'No, sir,' she said, and immediately wondered if that was the correct thing to say. Mr. Linden's head almost touched one of the ceiling beams, and when he went out of the kitchen door into the passage, he had to bend his head.

Kate was rather disappointed when Miss Nell placed a bowl of porridge before her and told her to help herself to sugar and cream. The bacon had smelt so delicious. But then Miss Nell said, 'When you've finished that there's an egg and bacon in the oven.

There's plenty of milk and you can finish off with an apple. There's no need to hurry over breakfast. We've got off to a good start this morning.'

It was pleasant sitting in the kitchen. Last night everything had seemed so strange, but now it all seemed friendly and comfortable. There was the big range with double ovens and four big kettles steaming on the stove, and a dresser so large that it occupied the whole of the wall opposite the window. It had four long shelves and on each of them were big blue and white plates, bowls, and vegetable dishes. Cups and jugs hung in rows from brass hooks. Standing on the dresser next to a box of cutlery and a pewter ink-stand was a vase of primroses, and Kate thought that it must have been Miss Nell who had placed the flowers in her bedroom to welcome her. She washed up the breakfast things and was putting the crockery back on the dresser when Miss Nell came downstairs again.

'Well done,' she said. 'Now you can go into the dairy to help Miss Grace.'

Miss Grace was busy with the butter. She explained that the skimmed milk had to go back to the farmyard for the pigs and calves and so Kate took a dipper and slowly filled two milk churns. Miss Grace showed her how to fix the lids on firmly. 'The boy from the yard will come for them later on,' she said.

All the utensils used in the dairy had to be scoured clean and then scalded with hot water, which meant a lot of walking to and from the scullery.

'Be careful that you don't scald yourself,' warned Miss Grace. 'Don't bring too much at a time.'

She told Kate how important it was that everything was properly scoured, otherwise the next lot of butter would be tainted. She inspected everything Kate washed and seemed quite pleased.

'Now I'm going upstairs to make the beds and tidy the bedrooms,' said Miss Grace. 'I want you to wash the floor with plenty of hot water. You'll find the brooms and brushes in that cupboard. When you have finished, Miss Nell will want you.'

While Kate was washing the floor, someone knocked at the door of the dairy and when she opened it, she found a boy of about fifteen standing there.

'I've come for the skimmed milk,' he said.

Kate remembered him from school. His name was Tom Collier, the biggest boy that Miss Crompton had ever caned.

'Didn't know you were working up here,' he said, as he wheeled the first churn outside.

'I only started this morning,' Kate said. She helped him to lift the churn on to the handcart and then Tom wheeled out the second churn and chained them both securely to the cart. He went off whistling, and Kate went back to her dairy floor. When she had finished her boots were splashed and her apron was rather wet, and when she went back into the kitchen she hoped that Miss Nell would not say anything. She was busy mixing pastry in a white bowl with a blue band round the top.

'We have our dinner at twelve o'clock,' she said, 'tea at four, and supper at eight. I'd like you to prepare the fruit and vegetables for me.'

She had put out potatoes, carrots, and cabbage, and a dish of cooking apples. Kate peeled the apples first, and Miss Nell came over to the table and took some of the peel.

'I love apple peel,' she said with a laugh.

When Kate had finished, Miss Nell inspected all the vegetables. An eye had been left in one of the potatoes, but otherwise everything was all right.

'Now you can tidy up in the dining-room,' said Miss Nell. 'You'll find an old black apron in the scullery to wear when you black-lead the grate.'

The dining room table was circular, made of walnut, and it shone with a warm satin glow. There were six chairs to match and a sideboard, where the cutlery, cruets, and the table-cloths and napkins were kept. Kate was still hard at work polishing the sideboard when Miss Nell came in and began to lay the table.

The three grown-ups had their meals in the dining-room, while Kate had hers by herself in the kitchen. She was glad of this. She thought that she could not have swallowed any food at all, sitting with the Master and Miss Nell and Miss Grace.

It had been a busy morning, and despite her large breakfast, she enjoyed the brown soup, the roast meat, and vegetables.

'Help yourself to cream,' said Miss Nell, when she gave her a big piece of apple pie. At home cream was considered to be a special treat, and Kate wished that her mother could have been there to share it with her. Mrs. Bassett always served herself last of all at meal-times, and sometimes she went without so that the children had as much to eat as they wanted.

Kate was quite glad to be able to sit down and rest. Her arms were stiff with so much carrying and polishing. She heard the Master go back to work, and soon after Miss Nell and Miss Grace came back with the dinner things from the dining-room.

'There's another piece of pie,' said Miss Nell, but Kate felt that she had already eaten too much. When she had finished washing up, she carried a can of hot water up the back stairs to her bedroom and washed and changed into one of Aunt Em's black dresses and put on a clean apron. When she came back into the kitchen, Miss Nell gave her some dusters to hem. Kate did not like sewing. Her stitches were always too large, Miss Crompton had said. She would really have liked to have taught the girls the embroidery work which she herself loved to do, but Lady Margaret had considered that plain sewing was really the more serviceable thing to learn. Kate preferred knitting. At home she knitted socks for her father and long stockings for Teddy and Jimmy.

Miss Nell took some crochet work from her sewing basket and began to work. Kate could see that it had a delicate shell-like pattern. She watched Miss Nell's busy fingers for a few minutes, and then Miss Nell looked up and said, 'Can you crochet, Kate?'

'No, Miss Nell,' said Kate.

'Would you like to learn?' said Miss Nell, and she found another steel crochet hook and a small ball of the fine cotton she was using and gave Kate her first lesson. At half past three Miss Nell said that it was time to start getting the tea, and she cut two platefuls of bread and butter while Kate made some toast. Miss Nell took a small teapot from the dresser cupboard. It was yellow with a brown handle and spout.

'This will be your own teapot,' she said. 'It holds just enough for two cups.'

They heard the Master coming in the back door for his tea, so Miss Nell carried the tray into the dining-room. After the tea things had been washed up, Miss Nell said that work was finished for the day. They would start getting the supper at quarter to eight. She gave Kate two books. One was a book of poems and the other was *Tales from Shakespeare* by Charles and Mary Lamb. Inside the front cover of each was written the name 'Ellen

Linden'. Kate sat at the table and began to read the book of stories from the Shakespeare plays. She forgot her surroundings, and she looked up with surprise when Miss Nell came into the kitchen and began preparing for supper. She had made out a list showing the order in which the day's work was to be done and pinned it on the side of the dresser.

When she was in bed, Kate began to see if she could memorize the list, but she only got as far as 'Clean boots and shoes' and then she was fast asleep. She had been too busy all day to be homesick.

Chapter 4

The next morning, Kate was awake at half past five. It felt rather strange to be the only person in the house to be up. Everything was silent, except for the noise her squeaky boots made as she went down the back stairs. She set to work, building up the fire in the range and filling the kettles from the pump and putting them on the range to boil. By the time she had filled the copper in the scullery the kettles were boiling, and she filled three brass cans with hot water. She took up the Master's and Miss Nell's first, and then came back for the can for Miss Grace. She thought that her voice sounded rather quivery when she called, 'Half past six, Master,' but Mr. Linden called back, 'Thank you, Kate,' in his deep, pleasant voice. She had to call out to Miss Grace twice before she answered, but when she knocked on Miss Nell's door, Miss Nell answered so promptly that Kate realized that she had been awake for some time and had probably been listening for the sound of her movements in the kitchen. She went back to light the fire under the copper and then she realized that she had not put the Master's boots outside his bedroom door, so she ran back upstairs with them. When she went back into the scullery the copper fire had gone out, and she relaid it, worrying all the time that Miss Nell would be coming downstairs and would find the fire still unlit. There was a pair of bellows hanging on a hook in the kitchen and she fetched them and began to pump the handles up and down. At last the fire sprang to life and she was able to make a start on cleaning the boots and shoes. Not long after, Miss Nell came into the scullery.

'Good morning, Kate,' she said. 'Is everything all right?'

'Yes, Miss Nell,' said Kate, silently praying that the copper fire was burning brightly. She held her breath as Miss Nell opened the door, and was relieved to see the leaping flames.

'Well done,' said Miss Nell, and went into the kitchen and began cooking the breakfast.

At the end of the day Kate was far less tired than she had been the day before, but as she sat alone in the kitchen in the evening she thought longingly of the cottage in the lane. She knew that at seven o'clock her mother would be cutting the bread for supper and pouring milk from the white jug with the gold rim round the

top which, with its muslin cover weighted with a fringe of blue beads, had been part of home for as long as she could ever remember. Thinking of her mother she felt her eyelids tremble and then there was a hot, sour taste in her throat and then she began to cry. Mingling with her sadness there was also the fear that Miss Nell would come in and be angry with her and perhaps she might be sent home. She thought of the brown tin trunk and the new boots and dresses. She knew how disappointed her mother and father would be and Aunt Em would have a lot to say about ungrateful girls who ought to know better than going round disgracing themselves and their families. After a while she was able to comfort herself with the thought that Sunday afternoon would soon come and then she would be able to go home and see everyone, and when Miss Nell came in and said that it was time to start getting the supper ready, she was calm again. Miss Nell saw the crumpled handkerchief in her lap and her red eyes, but she began to talk easily about the spring flowers in the back garden as if she had not even noticed Kate's homesickness. Kate was glad when supper was over and she was able to go to her room, but as she lay in bed she thought of the whispered conversations which she and Mary used to have before they went to sleep. Sometimes they laughed out loud, and then Mrs. Bassett would come up the stairs and tell them that it was late and that they must go to sleep or else they wouldn't be able to get up in the morning. It seems such a long time ago, Kate thought sadly.

By Thursday she had memorized the order of the list of work that Miss Nell had pinned up on the dresser, and she began to feel more at ease as each day passed. Her great fear was that she would not wake up in time, and consequently she was always awake far earlier than she need have been, but she found the extra few minutes especially useful when the fire under the copper wouldn't burn. She was always glad when Miss Nell came downstairs. When she was there, Kate thought that nothing could go wrong.

On Saturday evening the farm men came up to the house for their wages. There were fourteen men and Tom Collier, and they walked across the lawn to the window of the dining-room where the Master sat with the money on a tray. Miss Nell gave Kate a small envelope in which there were three shillings, her first week's wages. She had never seen so much money before, and she felt very rich.

On Sunday Mr. Hurford, the young farmer who was courting Miss Grace, came to dinner. Kate saw him from the scullery window when he and the Master walked out into the garden in their dark Sunday suits to smoke their pipes.

'Off you go, then, Kate,' said Miss Nell when all the washing-up was done, and Kate hurried upstairs and changed into her brown dress, thinking how strange it seemed not to have to put on a cap and apron. After she had buttoned her coat she stood before the mirror putting a hatpin in her hat, and she laughed at her reflection in the mirror when she saw that her cheeks were quite red with excitement and anticipation. She almost ran back down the stairs and after carefully closing the back door she hurried out into the lane and set out for the village. The sun was shining brightly and it seemed to Kate that never before had the fields and hedgerows seemed so fresh and green. When she reached the chapel her father and brothers and sisters were already there, and they made room for her in the varnished pew in which they were sitting. Kate was anxious to go home to see her mother, but the circuit minister had been unable to come to Bretherton on that Sunday and so the service was conducted by Mr. Fawkes, the wheelwright, whose sermons were always at least fifteen minutes longer than those of the minister. She thought that even the hymns that had been chosen must be the longest in the hymn-book, but at last the service came to an end and the rather restless congregation was able to stream out into the warm Sunday afternoon.

'Is everything all right?' asked Mr. Bassett, looking at her intently.

'Yes,' said Kate with a smile, and Mr. Bassett gave a little nod of satisfaction.

Her mother gave her a big hug when she ran into the kitchen.

'You seem to have grown, Kate,' she said, and Kate thought that perhaps Mrs. Bassett was right. Somehow the kitchen seemed smaller than how she remembered it.

It should have been the Sunday for Aunt Em's visit, but she had called the evening before to say that Uncle Percy's mother had not been well, and she supposed she ought to go over to her cottage at Ditton and put things to rights.

'If I don't,' Aunt Em had said grimly, 'no one else will. I'm sorry to have to miss seeing Kate, but tell her that I hope that she's getting on all right.'

To Kate it hardly seemed possible that it was only a week ago since she had sat at the table hoping that she would not cry and disgrace herself in front of the little ones. Mary wanted to know all about Penrose Farm, and Kate told her about the kitchen with the pump, the dining-room with the big, round table, and the drawing-room with the velvet armchairs and the thick carpet. She told her about the dresser and the linen cupboard, and about Miss Nell, Miss Grace, and the Master, and Mary thought that it must be wonderful to be able to go out to work and not to have to go to school any more where Miss Crompton seemed to be crosser than ever.

When Kate was helping her mother with the washing-up, Mrs. Bassett told her that although they had enjoyed hearing about the furnishings at Penrose Farm, she must be careful not to gossip about the people for whom she worked.

'You are living in their home, and they trust you,' she said. 'Make sure that you don't break that trust.'

'Yes,' said Kate. 'I know what you mean,' and she resolved to be careful in the future. Rather shyly she took her wages from the pocket of her coat. The money was still in the small brown envelope.

'I'd like you to have this,' she said.

'That's very kind of you, Kate,' her mother said, 'but this is your money which you have earned. You keep it and save it. When you've saved up ten shillings, you can put it in the post office and have a bank book. You'll need things. Clothes always seem to be wearing out, and boots don't last very long. As you get older you'll find that it is a good thing to have some money put by.'

After the twins had eaten their supper, Kate took them upstairs and tucked them up in bed. She kissed them good night, and then opened the door of the bedroom she had shared with Mary and stood looking in. This room, too, seemed smaller than she remembered. She looked at the shelf which her father had made for her so that she had somewhere to keep her treasures. It was empty, because her few possessions were on the dressing-table in the attic at Penrose Farm. When she glanced at what she had always thought of as her side of the bed, she saw that Rose's night-gown now lay there next to Mary's on the coverlet, and a strange feeling of loneliness swept over her. It's almost as if I had gone away for ever, she thought sadly. As she went slowly down the stairs she could hear the others in the parlour playing a game of 'I Spy', and she went quietly in and sat down, not saying anything.

'Let Kate have a turn,' said Mrs. Bassett after a while.

'Yes, come on, Kate,' said Mary, and so she was drawn back into the family group. During the game she tried to pretend that everything was just the same as it always had been, but it did not seem very long before Mrs. Bassett looked at the clock and said, 'It's time you started back, Kate.'

'Just five more minutes,' she said, and her mother nodded and went out into the pantry and cut her a slice of cake. When the game was over Kate went into the passage and put on her hat and coat.

'Good-bye, then,' she said a little breathlessly.

'Good-bye, lass,' said her father, and Kate kissed Mary, Rose, and Teddy. Mrs. Bassett went with her to the gate.

'We'll see you again on Sunday,' she said.

'Yes,' said Kate heavily.

As she walked back to the farm she thought that the journey seemed much longer than it had that afternoon, and she realized that it must be because every step this time was taking her away from home, and not bringing her nearer to it. She tried to forget the strange, cold feeling that she had when she saw that Rose was now sharing the bedroom with Mary, but it seemed to her that she was now no longer part of the life of home. Everything was going on in the same comfortable way, but she could no longer be there. If only I could go back, she thought, and not have to worry any more about lighting that copper fire.

When she reached Penrose Farm, Miss Nell was in the kitchen preparing the supper.

'Did you have a nice time, Kate?' she asked.

'Oh yes, Miss Nell,' said Kate, but her voice trembled.

'And Sunday will soon come round again,' said Miss Nell.

Mr. Hurford was still there, so Kate laid four places in the dining-room for supper. She wondered if any young man was courting Miss Nell.

After supper Miss Nell and Kate sorted out the sheets, pillowcases, towels, and clothes which needed washing and put them to soak in two zinc tubs of water, ready for Mrs. Maslen, a washerwoman from the village, who came to the farm at eight

39

o'clock the next morning. She was a short, fat woman, wearing a dark green overall and a man's cap. Kate thought that she had never seen anyone with such big, red hands and arms. Mrs. Maslen went into the scullery and soon it was full of steam with moisture running down the walls, but she worked steadily on with no apparent discomfort, poking the clothes boiling in the copper with a thick stick. At twelve o'clock she came back into the kitchen to have her dinner with Kate. She sat down at the table still wearing the man's cap and looked appreciatively at the meal which Kate put in front of her.

'I always say that they keep a good table at Penrose Farm,' she said. 'That Miss Nell is just like her mother. It was just the same when Mrs. Linden was alive. Always plenty to eat. Not like some of the places I go to, where they don't put out enough for even a bird to fill up on.'

'How long has Mrs. Linden been dead?' asked Kate.

'About ten years, I should think,' said Mrs. Maslen. 'Miss Nell was about fifteen at the time. Mrs. Linden was a fine-looking woman, and her two girls take after her. She didn't come from round these parts, though. She came from somewhere in Derbyshire.'

Mrs. Maslen spent six days of the week washing and ironing, going to various houses in the district. She also did some work for Lady Margaret, and every Wednesday one of the grooms would bring the laundry in a locked trunk to her cottage. There were two keys to the trunk. One was held by the housekeeper at Ellswood Park, and Mrs. Maslen wore the other key on a piece of string round her neck. The groom came to fetch the trunk again on Saturday morning.

'I've been washing and ironing for the Park this twelve years,' Mrs. Maslen told Kate, 'and in all that time I've never sent anything back with a scorch mark or even a speck of iron mould. Still, I don't suppose I should have kept the job all that time if I had.'

After she had eaten her dinner, Mrs. Maslen went back into the scullery and Kate could hear the creaking noise of the mangle. At the end of the day she realized how hard Mrs. Maslen must have worked when she saw the four long lines of washing hung out to dry.

'It'll be a good day for drying, that's a blessing,' said the

40

washerwoman. 'There's one thing I can't abide, and that's a wet washing day and a body trying to get clothes dry indoors. To my mind it never comes up such a good colour.'

She came the next day to do the ironing, using six flat-irons of differing sizes which were kept heating on the kitchen range. The largest was so big that Kate wondered how anyone could manage to lift it, but Mrs. Maslen used it as if it had been as light as the smallest iron which was about the size of Kate's hands. She thought how marvellous it must be to be able to iron so smoothly and quickly as Mrs. Maslen.

'Each of us to our trade,' said the washerwoman, when she saw that Kate was watching her, but she was pleased by the admiring expression on Kate's face. Nothing seemed difficult to her, not even the Master's shirts nor the frills on Miss Grace's blouses. As she worked, the kitchen was filled with the scent of the freshly ironed clothes, which, for some unknown reason, always made Kate think of summer. When everything was done, Mrs. Maslen sat down and put her feet up on a stool.

'When you've been on your feet all day, you begin to find it at my age,' she said. Kate then realized that in addition to the man's cap on her head, Mrs. Maslen was wearing a pair of men's boots on her feet. Surprise must have shown in her face because Mrs. Maslen explained that she wore an old pair of her husband's boots because they were broad-fitting and comfortable.

'My feet were fair crippled in my own boots,' she said, 'but since I've been wearing a pair of my man's, I've been as right as a trivet.'

She told Kate that she had a married son who worked for the miller at Chaxton and a daughter who was in service in Manchester.

'I said to her, I can't think for the life of me why you want to go gallivanting all up the country like that. There must be plenty of places round these parts. She would have her way though, and off she goes, and I don't see hide nor hair of her until she has a holiday. Still, she's a good girl, though I do say it as shouldn't, and she always writes home regular once a fortnight.'

Miss Nell had said that when Mrs. Maslen had finished her work she was to have a cup of tea, and though it was only three o'clock, Kate made the tea in her own special teapot. As it was too hot, Mrs. Maslen poured the tea into her saucer.

'You make a good cup of tea, I must say,' she said. 'You've got a good place here with that Miss Nell. Mind you look after yourself. I'll see you in a fortnight's time,' she went on, as she put on her coat and pulled the man's cap straight on her head. 'Let's hope the weather will be fine.'

Some afternoons Kate went with Miss Grace through the gate in the back garden wall and across the field which led to the farm buildings to collect the eggs. In the yard there were five grey geese who always started hissing and flapping their wings in a threatening manner. Kate was afraid of them, but Miss Grace always walked by calmly, and Kate tried to do the same, although she felt that she would have preferred to have run past. If any of the men were in the farmyard, they touched their caps respectfully, and Miss Grace smiled and wished them good afternoon. Tom Collier, the boy who came up to the house to collect the skimmed milk, always gave Kate a cheerful grin. When all the eggs had been collected, they had to be washed, and Kate was always glad when this task was done because she was afraid of breaking them. She continued to have her crochet lessons with Miss Nell and she was making good progress. Miss Nell told her that in the evenings she could borrow any of the books in the drawing-room bookcase.

'Miss Grace and I had them when we were at school,' she said with a smile, 'but I don't think that you will find them too old-fashioned.'

One afternoon Kate and Miss Nell went out into the fields to pick dandelions because Miss Nell wanted to make some dandelion wine. She found a pair of cotton gloves for Kate so that she would not stain her hands, and also an old sunbonnet. It was the first time that Kate had ever possessed a pair of gloves, and she felt quite elegant wearing them. The sunbonnet had a little pleated curtain at the back to shield her neck from the sun. Miss Nell had put a fresh blue ribbon round her big, straw hat, and Kate thought how cool and charming she looked in her blue dress and long white apron. Miss Nell lined two wicker baskets with newspaper and they set off.

'I think we'll go to the fields down by the copse,' said Miss Nell. 'We might find some bluebells.'

When they reached the stone stile which led into the field, a man was standing there. He was wearing a short jacket, breeches, and highly polished boots and leggings. A gun lay at his feet, and Kate thought that he must be a gamekeeper.

'Good afternoon,' said the man, taking off his hat.

'Good afternoon,' replied Miss Nell. She turned to Kate. 'Would you like to go and start picking, Kate? I'll join you in a few minutes.'

Kate had never before realized how difficult it was to climb over a stile with two people watching, but the man helped her while Miss Nell held the two baskets. As she began to pick the dandelions she wondered why the gamekeeper was on the land belonging to Penrose Farm. She was not even sure that he was a gamekeeper at all. He had not been like Aunt Em's husband whose sharp eyes seemed to see everything, and although the stranger had a gun, he was not wearing the kind of dark brown corduroy jacket that Uncle Percy always wore.

It was pleasant to be out in the field and gradually the baskets began to be filled with the bright yellow heads of the dandelions. All around were the drowsy sounds of a summer afternoon. Everything seemed to shimmer in the sunlight. A cuckoo called from a nearby tree and there were strange, quick movements in the hedge. A butterfly hovered over a tall moon daisy so close to Kate that she stayed quite still until it flew on. The field was on slightly higher ground than the land surrounding it and she could look down and see the tall grass ready for mowing in a few days' time. 'Another week if the weather holds,' the Master had said. The summer breeze moved through the grass like a ribbon of silver and Kate thought how good it was to be out in the open. It was almost like a holiday.

Miss Nell had still not come into the field even when both baskets were full, so Kate went into the copse to look for blue-bells. Under the branches of the hazel-nut trees the air was fresh and cool. The bluebells were in full bloom and they seemed to rise like blue smoke round the trees. Kate picked a handful of flowers and then came out of the copse. She saw that Miss Nell was sitting beside the two baskets.

'I was detained, Kate,' she said, 'and now it seems that you've done all the work. What a beautiful day it is!'

The fine June weather continued and the Master and his men were able to start haymaking on the day that he had planned. The brewer from Chaxton delivered a large barrel of beer to the

43

kitchen door and a space was made for it in the pantry. Miss Nell brought three large stone jars in wicker baskets down from the attic next to Kate's and after tea she filled them from the barrel and tied two enamel mugs to the neck of each of them. At about six o'clock Miss Grace and Kate carried the stone jars out to the trap and drove down to the hayfields. Miss Grace tethered the pony to the gate and she and Kate carried the jars into the field and placed them under the hedge. The Master and all the farm men were there, wearing old straw hats and with the sleeves of their shirts rolled up, their faces and arms reddened by the sun. The grass in the first field had been cut two days earlier and the men were spread out in a long line tossing it with pitchforks so that it would dry as quickly as possible. In the next field the grass was being cut by a horse-drawn mowing machine, and to Kate it seemed just a little sad that at one moment the grass was waving in the breeze, a tangle of sorrel, buttercups, and moon daisies, and then after the mowing machine with the drover guiding the horses had passed by, it lay in flat green furrows, almost as if the Angel of Death had passed over, as in the story in the Book of Exodus. When the men saw Miss Grace and Kate standing there, they all came over to the hedge for a mug of beer, touching their battered straw hats in deference to Miss Grace and smiling at Kate, their teeth showing very white against their sunburnt faces. When the Master, the cowman, and the shepherd poured the beer into the mugs, Kate saw that they lifted the heavy jars as easily as if they had been empty.

'It's main dry work, this haymaking,' said one of the farm men. 'And we're much obliged to you, Master, I'm sure. Here's to you, Miss Grace, and yours.'

Miss Grace smiled and coloured slightly, and Kate knew that the man was referring to Mr. Hurford. Tom Collier had a sip from one of the mugs, made a wry face, and then handed it back to the shepherd.

'I reckon I'll stick to my bottle of cold tea,' he said, as the men laughed.

'Wise lad, Tom,' said the Master.

Kate noticed that the Master waited until all the men had a mug of beer before he poured a drink for himself.

'We'll be on until about eight or half past, Grace,' he said. 'Don't wait supper for me.'

44

'All right, Father,' said Miss Grace. She and Kate watched him as he walked back to the line of men, a big, square figure against the blue sky.

On the way back to the farm, Miss Grace told Kate to take the reins.

'I can't drive,' said Kate nervously. Before she had come to Penrose Farm, she had never even ridden in a trap.

'All the more reason to start now,' said Miss Grace with a laugh, and she put the reins into Kate's hands.

'Firmly but gently,' she said.

Kate held herself very stiffly at first, afraid that Ladybird, the pony, would suddenly bolt and throw both Miss Grace and herself right out of the trap into the hedge just where the stinging nettles were at their highest. But Ladybird, as if sensing Kate's uneasiness, gave a little whinny of encouragement, which made her laugh, and as they went along the lane to the farmhouse, she found that she rather liked driving the trap. Miss Grace sat back with her arms comfortably folded and smiled.

Chapter 5

Miss Grace and Mr. Hurford were to be married in the third week of July, and Miss Grace was busy preparing for the move to her new home, Ringstone Farm, which was nine miles from Bretherton. One afternoon she and Kate drove into Chaxton to do some shopping. Wedding presents were beginning to arrive for Miss Grace, and Kate thought that she, too, would like to give her a wedding gift. She knew that there was something special about them. At home in the parlour there was a picture of swans on a lake which Mrs. Bassett often said had been a present from the lady for whom she had worked until she left to be married. There was also a lustre jug which had been the gift of Mr. Bassett's mother who had died soon after Kate was born. Kate had decided that she would crochet a set of dressing-table mats for Miss Grace.

With Miss Grace to lead the way, she found that the shops were not so overwhelming as she had thought when she went to Chaxton to take the Labour Examination. When they went into Billington's, the drapery shop, the man in a long, black tailcoat came hurrying forward with a chair for Miss Grace to sit on, and clicked his fingers at one of the assistants, who stepped forward with a pleasant smile on her face. While Miss Grace was looking at sheets and pillow-cases, Kate went to the counter where the crochet cotton was sold, and was attended to by a rather sad-faced girl in a black dress and a narrow white collar. Kate wondered what it would be like to work in a shop. It must be rather pleasant to see so many pretty things, she thought, but then she remembered that Nancy had said that all the girls had to live in over the shop and the housekeeper kept the girls short of food. She decided that she did not like the man in the long, black tailcoat who watched the assistants very closely as they went about their work.

The girl who served Kate was very helpful, showing her crochet cotton in various colours. Kate decided that she would make the mats in white, so that they would not clash with any colour scheme which Miss Grace had chosen.

'If you have any left over, you can always use it for lace edgings,' said the assistant as she tied the parcel. When Kate went back to Miss Grace she was busy looking at lace curtaining. She looked at a roll of fawn-coloured lace and at a roll of white, and Kate held her breath while Miss Grace considered which to have. She finally chose the white lace, and Kate sighed almost audibly in relief.

'May we transport the parcels to your carriage, madam?' said the man in the black tailcoat.

'Could they be taken to the livery stables at the Rose and Crown?' said Miss Grace. 'We have some other shopping to do now.'

'Certainly, madam,' said the man. 'It will be no trouble at all.'

'We shall be leaving at about half past four,' said Miss Grace.

'Very good, madam. They will be delivered to the Rose and Crown straight away.'

The man opened the door of the shop with a flourish and bowed as Miss Grace and Kate went out into the street. Kate looked back and saw that the sad-faced girl was beginning to gather up the bulky parcels.

In the weeks that Kate had been at Penrose Farm she had not spent very much of her wages and had managed to save up ten shillings which Mrs. Bassett had thought was a good round figure with which to open an account at the savings bank, so while Miss Grace went into a china shop, Kate went to open the account at the post office. She had the money wrapped in one of the brown envelopes in which she received her wages.

'I'd like to open an account,' she said to the man behind the wire grille.

'Certainly,' said the clerk.

Kate felt a little sad when the man took the money and gave her in return a bank book with her name on it. He smiled.

'Missing your money already?' he said. 'It's safer with the Government than it is in an old teapot at home, you know. And you'll be getting interest on your money, too. Bring some money in every month and you'll have a nice little nest egg for your bottom drawer.'

Kate smiled and put the bank book in the pocket of her dress

and went back to the china shop. Miss Grace was just coming out.
'That didn't take as long as I expected,' she said. 'If you've
done all that you wanted to do, Kate, we'll have a cup of tea
before we go back.'

Kate had never before been in a teashop, and she felt a little
uneasy as she followed Miss Grace into the Willow Pattern Tea
Rooms. Most of the small tables were occupied by smartly
dressed women in light-coloured dresses and large hats, and she
was glad that Miss Grace chose a table in an alcove and that she
was able to sit with her back to the rest of the room. She hoped
that she would not make a noise when she drank her tea, and she
decided that she would not have anything to eat because she was
afraid that the food might stick in her throat and that she would
have a fit of coughing and embarrass Miss Grace by drawing
attention to herself.

Her heart sank when a waitress came to the table and Miss
Grace ordered buttered toast and small iced cakes, but once the
ordering was done, Miss Grace began to talk in her pleasant,
easy manner about the things she had bought, and when the tea
came, Kate found that she was able to enjoy the food. It seemed
strange to be sitting down with Miss Grace pouring out the tea,
and because she had not had to make it herself, it seemed to Kate
that it was the most refreshing cup she had ever tasted.

When they went back to the livery stables at the Rose and
Crown, all the parcels had been delivered and as they drove home,
Kate thought about the sad-faced girl at Billington's. She could
not really think of the talkative Nancy working there.

One morning after the work in the dairy was finished, Miss
Grace packed some food into a hamper and she and Kate carried
a trunk containing some of her things downstairs and put it into
the trap. Some of the new furniture had been delivered to
Ringstone Farm and they were going to arrange everything as
Miss Grace wished. Mrs. Bray, the cowman's wife, went with
them.

'You can take the reins, Kate,' said Miss Grace, so Kate sat in
the front of the trap and Mrs. Bray sat in the back with the hamper
and the trunk. This was the first time that Kate had ever driven
on the main road, but they met only a few carts coming very
slowly from the fields. The road to Ringstone Farm went past
South Lodge, and as they went by Aunt Em was just opening the

gates for Lady Margaret, who was sitting very erectly in her carriage. It was Wednesday, and Kate guessed that she was on her way to the school to call the register. The groom was the same man who had been standing by the stile on the afternoon that she and Miss Nell had gone to pick dandelions.

Lady Margaret bowed stiffly to Miss Grace, who bowed in return, while the groom raised his whip in salute as they passed. Aunt Em stared at Kate when she saw her holding the reins.

'Good morning, Aunt Em,' called Kate, as the trap went by.

'Morning,' said Aunt Em, grudgingly. She stood and watched the trap until it was out of sight, and then went back indoors feeling in a very bad temper which was not improved when an hour later she looked out of the kitchen window and saw that the clothes-line had broken and that two sheets and a pillow-case lay on the ground. As she grimly relit the copper fire in the scullery she thought that it was all very fine for some folk driving round the countryside when they ought to have been hard at work earning their living.

Ringstone Farm stood at the foot of the downs just below the spot where a circle of eight black stones stood starkly against the skyline. Kate remembered that once during a scripture lesson the vicar had said that the stones were very old and had been there since prehistoric times.

The farmhouse was not as large as that of Penrose Farm, but it had the same welcoming air. In the front garden there was a cedar tree which made Kate think of King Solomon and the building of the temple.

Miss Grace carried the hamper and Kate and Mrs. Bray followed behind with the trunk. Miss Grace unlocked the front door and said in a proud, happy voice, 'Welcome to Ringstone Farm', and the hamper and trunk were deposited in the kitchen and then Miss Grace showed Kate and Mrs. Bray the house. There was so much to admire. There was a black and white tiled hall, and all the rooms were large with high ceilings. In the dining-room were the tables and six chairs which formed the Master's wedding gift to Miss Grace.

"'Tis lovely,' said Mrs. Bray. 'Did you ever see such carving on the backs of those chairs. And that carpet!'

Kate liked the drawing-room with its sofa and wing armchairs in fawn-coloured velvet. Under the window was a long window seat with a hinged lid which also served as a chest. Upstairs there were four bedrooms and a small attic. In Miss Grace's room there was a pretty walnut dressing-table and Kate thought how well the mats she was making would look on its light, polished surface. Another two evenings and they would be finished.

They spent a busy morning. Mrs. Bray scrubbed the attic floorboards, Kate polished all the furniture, and Miss Grace hung the curtains in all the rooms. Although Mr. Hurford was already farming the land at Ringstone Farm, he was still living at home with his parents and sister two miles away, but that day it had been arranged that he would have dinner with Miss Grace, and when he came at twelve o'clock, a meal was set out for them in the dining-room, while Kate and Mrs. Bray had theirs in the kitchen. Miss Grace had brought ham, cheese, cold potatoes, lettuce, and cucumber, and an apple pie.

'They do say that work's the best appetizer,' said Mrs. Bray, and Kate agreed, surprised to find how hungry she was.

'They make a smart-looking couple,' said Mrs. Bray, when Mr.

Hurford and Miss Grace walked out into the orchard. 'I always look forward to a wedding. The last one I remember—it must be all of four years ago—was when Miss Louise from Ellswood Park was married. Such a dress! It was made by a dressmaker in London. Pity that Miss Louise takes after her mother, Lady Margaret, in looks. They say that she's as different to her mother as chalk is to cheese in her ways, though. And just as well. That Lady Margaret can be a proper tartar and no mistake. It's her son, Sir Edward, that has got all the looks, just like his father before him.'

Kate said that she didn't think that she had ever seen either Miss Louise or Sir Edward.

'Well, I don't suppose you would see Miss Louise now she's married. She lives in some big house up in London,' said Mrs. Bray. 'But we saw Sir Edward with Lady Margaret this morning.'

At that moment Miss Grace came into the kitchen with her dinner tray and Mrs. Bray's conversation ended. In the afternoon as Kate unpacked the sheets and pillow-cases from Miss Grace's trunk, she thought about what Mrs. Bray had said. She remembered the afternoon that she and Miss Nell had gone to pick dandelions and the man had been standing by the stile. She had thought that perhaps he had been a gamekeeper from Ellswood Park, when he had in fact been Sir Edward himself.

In all the excitement of the preparations for Miss Grace's wedding, Kate had thought of Miss Nell and she had supposed that she, too, would one day marry and leave Penrose Farm. She realized that as yet, no one seemed to be courting Miss Nell. No young farmer ever came to dinner on Sunday as Mr. Hurford did. As she thought of Miss Nell's meeting with Sir Edward, Kate wondered if perhaps he was the man whom one day Miss Nell would marry. Then she remembered what Aunt Em had said.

'Not that the Lindens are what I call real gentry—not like they are up at Ellswood Park. Farmer Linden works alongside his men—and he only rents Penrose Farm.'

She went thoughtfully down the stairs. In the kitchen Miss Grace had hung up white, blue-spotted curtains at the window and tacked a short blue plush curtain round the mantelpiece. Mrs. Bray had cleaned the kitchen range and laid the fire ready, and there was a red geranium in a flower pot on the window sill and a towel on a roller behind the door. Miss Grace had already put some of the best china in the cabinet in the drawing-room and now she was beginning to unpack the china for everyday use. Mrs. Bray and Kate admired everything as it was unwrapped. They stayed at the farmhouse until half past four, and then drove home well pleased with all the work they had done. The day's work was not so very different from what would normally have been done at Penrose Farm, but because everything was new and there was the excitement of getting the house ready, it seemed to Kate almost like a holiday. Miss Grace again allowed her to drive back along the quiet dusty roads and the lanes with banks tangled high with cow parsley and pink campions. As they passed South Lodge, Kate was relieved when she saw that Aunt Em was nowhere to be seen. She knew that she would have a great deal to say the next time she visited Mrs. Bassett.

The crocheted dressing-table mats were at last finished, and Kate wrapped them in tissue paper and gave them to Miss Grace. All the wedding presents were displayed on the sideboard in the dining-room and on two tables in the hall. They were all useful gifts because most of Miss Grace's friends and relatives were farming people and there were oil lamps, cutlery, sheets and pillow-cases, china and glassware, and two large piles of towels and table-cloths. A few of her friends had realized that there should be room in every house for something beautiful and ornamental and there was a statue in green-tinted Parian ware and two porcelain figures of a shepherd and a shepherdess. From Miss Nell there was a sewing chair with a blue velvet seat, and also a green and gold dinner service. Kate felt that her own gift seemed rather small, and she felt rather shy as she gave the little parcel to Miss Grace. Both she and Miss Nell admired the intricate pattern.

'Crochet work was something I could never master,' said Miss Grace. 'Thank you very much, Kate.'

On the morning of Miss Grace's wedding day, Kate pulled back her bedroom curtains at half past five and looked out of the window, smiling when she saw the mist above the fields, relieved that it was the promise of a fine day. When she went upstairs with a can of hot water for Miss Grace, she had only to knock on the bedroom door once and Miss Grace answered as if she had been awake for some time. Although it was the day of the wedding, the work of the farm had to go on, and Miss Nell and Miss Grace came down at the usual time, and the Master went out to the yard. Miss Nell had asked Mrs. Bray and the shepherd's wife, Mrs. Crewe, to be at the farmhouse at eight o'clock, and they arrived together.

'Happy the bride the sun shines on,' said Mrs. Bray, as she and Mrs. Crewe put on their overalls.

The wedding was to be at two o'clock. Fifty guests were invited and it had been decided that the reception would be held on the front lawn. Two of the farm men set up the long trestle tables and carried out all the available chairs from the house, together with the long benches which had been hired from Chaxton and which were brought by the baker when he arrived with the wedding cake, a basket of loaves and rolls, and two big trays of cakes. While Miss Nell, Miss Grace, and Mrs. Bray prepared the food, Kate and Mrs. Crewe washed all the cups and saucers and plates and glassware. As they would be so busy, it was decided that they would have what Miss Nell called 'a standing-up dinner' of bread and cheese, but a plate of ham and mashed potato and pickles was put in the dining-room for the Master when he came home at twelve o'clock.

'The excitement fair takes your breath away,' said Mrs. Bray. 'Did you ever see such a spread?' she went on, looking round the kitchen.

Everything was ready by half past twelve, and then Miss Grace and Miss Nell went upstairs to dress for the wedding. After Kate had changed into her black afternoon dress and Mrs. Bray and Mrs. Crewe exchanged their overalls for clean white aprons, they went into the hall and waited for Miss Grace. The Master was there, very smart in his dark suit, and wearing a big white button-hole. When Miss Grace came down the stairs she looked so beautiful that Kate wanted to cry. She thought that if ever she was married she would have a white silk dress with a long, flowing skirt and a veil of fine lace exactly the same as Miss Grace was wearing. Her bouquet was a small spray of rosebuds.

'Well, Grace,' said the Master. That was all he said, but his voice was full with pride and love. Miss Nell's dress was pale blue, and with it she wore a big blue picture hat and carried a posy of cream-coloured roses.

'My stars,' said Mrs. Bray. 'You both look a real picture and no mistake.'

As soon as they had driven off to the church, Kate, Mrs. Bray, and Mrs. Crewe began to lay the tables. The shepherd's wife was a very quiet person who spoke almost in a whisper.

'Such a bride,' she said to Kate, 'and a grand day for a wedding, too. There's not so much as a breeze to ruffle up the tablecloths.'

When everything was ready, Kate and the two women stood looking at their handiwork. Miss Grace had arranged pink roses in glass vases and these were set at intervals all down the long tables. All the food was covered with small white cloths which would be taken off as soon as the guests began to arrive. The wedding cake stood on a big silver stand with a garland of ferns and roses round the base, and there was a separate table where all the cups and saucers were set out. Tom Collier was perched up in a tall elm tree and he came scrambling down as soon as he saw the first pony trap in the distance and ran to tell Mrs. Crewe, who hurried into the kitchen to make the tea in four large teapots. Miss Grace and Mr. Hurford came into the garden looking very happy, and they stood by the gate and greeted the guests as they arrived. The Master walked in with a small lady on his arm, whom Kate knew at once must be Mr. Hurford's mother because they looked so alike, and Miss Nell came in with old Mr. Hurford whose buttonhole seemed to be the largest of all. More and more people began to arrive and soon the garden seemed to be filled with men in dark suits and women wearing light-coloured dresses and big hats and carrying parasols. Kate saw that Miss Nell glanced at the tables and then smiled, pleased that everything had been arranged just as she and Miss Grace had planned. Soon the guests were seated and Mrs. Crewe was pouring tea for Kate and Mrs. Bray to hand round, while the Master and Mr. Hurford's father carried round big jugs of beer and cider. When the wedding cake had been cut and the speeches had been made, people began to move round forming small groups, and Miss Nell went round speaking to everyone, indicating with a small smile and a nod of her head whose plate was empty and which glass needed refilling. Although she was kept busy, Kate enjoyed the afternoon, proud that everything had been done as Miss Nell had wished. The time passed so quickly that Kate was surprised when Miss Grace went upstairs to change and came down later wearing a smart grey costume and a white hat. She still carried the spray of rosebuds, which she was going to place on her mother's grave. Everyone crowded round the trap, laughing and waving as Miss Grace and Mr. Hurford drove away, and soon after, the guests began to leave and Miss Nell and the Master stood at the gate, shaking hands with everyone as they left. The house and garden seemed very quiet when everyone had gone, and then Miss Nell changed into her print dress and white apron and helped to clear everything away.

It was seven o'clock when everything was tidied up, the glassware and china washed, and the trestle tables and benches stacked against the scullery wall, and then Miss Nell cut pieces of wedding cake and poured glasses of sherry for Kate, Mrs. Bray, and Mrs. Crewe.

'Here's to Miss Grace, then,' said Mrs. Bray, 'and may she have good luck and good fortune all her married life.'

'Yes,' echoed Mrs. Crewe, made bold by all the excitement and the wine. 'And may it be your turn soon, Miss Nell.'

'Thank you,' said Miss Nell, but there was a certain sadness in her smile, and Kate wondered if she was thinking of Sir Edward.

There was still a lot of food left over from the wedding reception and Miss Nell filled a basket each for Mrs. Bray and Mrs. Crewe. When they had gone she said, 'After all the excitement, Kate, I think I'd like to go for a drive and get some fresh air. Perhaps your mother could use up some of this food for me. We don't want to be eating leftovers for the rest of the week. We'll drive down to the village and you can spend an hour at home.'

Mrs. Bassett was very pleased with the basket of food which Kate took home. As well as cakes and sandwiches, Miss Nell had sent a large slice of wedding cake decorated with white sugar roses.

'Tell us all about the wedding,' urged Mary.

Remembering what Mrs. Bassett had said about gossiping about her employers, Kate glanced at her mother, but Mrs. Bassett smiled and said, 'Yes, do, Kate. Everyone loves a wedding,' and so she described all the events of the afternoon. The hour passed quickly and Teddy came running in to say that there was a lady in a trap waiting at the gate outside.

'Did you enjoy your drive, Miss Nell?' asked Kate, as she climbed up into the trap.

'Yes,' she said, 'and I found some honeysuckle.'

When they were back at the farm she arranged the sprays of blossom in a vase. Kate knew that Miss Nell liked to see flowers on the dresser in the kitchen and she thought that she would put them there as she usually did, but this time Miss Nell carried the vase upstairs to her own room.

Chapter 6

The boys and girls who attended the parish church at Bretherton often pitied the children who went to the chapel in Green Lane. Nothing ever seemed to happen there. It was so different at the church, where there were so many events to look forward to. Early in the year there was the Rogation service, when the vicar and the choir walked in procession in their white surplices and purple cassocks for an open-air service at Glebe Farm, where the farm implements and the fields were blessed. There was the special service on Mothering Sunday when the children were given spring flowers from the vicarage garden to present to their mothers. In July there was the summer picnic on the vicarage lawn, followed by races and a treasure hunt arranged by the churchwardens. At the Harvest Festival, the display of fruit and vegetables in the church was always far more impressive than that at the chapel. The broad stone window sills would be decorated with peaches and grapes sent by Lady Margaret from the greenhouses at Ellswood Park, and in the chancel there would be flowers and shrubs from her own conservatory. In the chapel there would be flowers and vegetables from the village gardens. In October there was the service of Confirmation, when the bishop came from Chaxton to confirm twenty boys and girls. He was an awe-inspiring figure in his satin cope and embroidered mitre. The boys who were going to be confirmed sat in the front pews dressed in their Sunday suits, and the girls sat behind them wearing white dresses and veils. No chapel girl would ever know the delightful excitement of wearing a white veil at the age of fourteen. At Christmas-time there was the church carol-singing party who visited all the houses in the village, and sometimes they were asked inside to have slices of fruit cake and cups of cocoa. For the children there was the Sunday school tea party in the parish hall, when the vicar's wife, Mrs. Willis, and his daughters, Miss Ruth and Miss Elizabeth, borrowed long white aprons from the cook from the vicarage kitchen and handed round plates of sandwiches and buns and poured tea from tall, white enamelled jugs.

'There's always something going on at the church,' Jessie Banks said, 'but you don't seem to do anything at the chapel, Kate.'

'There's always the anniversary,' said Kate, loyally, and to her it was the most important event in Bretherton. It was always a great occasion. The children learned special hymns and poems and Mr. Blease practised special pieces of music on the old harmonium. Everyone wore a flower or spray in his buttonhole, and after the service they all sat down to tea in the small schoolroom behind the chapel. Mrs. Hawkins, who taught the children the anniversary hymns and songs, liked only the clear treble of children's voices, and so Kate, whose voice would one day be a deep, vibrant contralto, never sat on the platform with the children who sang in the choir. Instead, Mrs. Hawkins allowed her to give one of the Bible readings, and sometimes she recited a thanksgiving poem which the minister had written. Both Mary and Teddy were in Mrs. Hawkins' choir, and Mary often sang one of the solos. Her voice had a purity which brought tears to the eyes of the older people in the congregation. In her special position as aunt of the soloist, Aunt Em had once gone to the chapel anniversary service simply to hear Mary sing. It was only the second time that she had attended a chapel. The first time was when Kate's mother and father had been married at Malmesbury. Even then Aunt Em had not been impressed.

'Such a bare, poor-looking place,' she said to Uncle Percy, when she described the wedding to him. 'No stained-glass windows and no cloth on the altar. No font and no organ. Nothing religious at all, really. Of course, they did have a Bible, otherwise we might just as well have been in a barn.'

She thought that the chapel in Green Lane was equally bare and poor.

'Whitewash on the walls and not a decent hassock for anyone to kneel on,' she said. 'Still, it was no more than what I expected.'

The anniversary was in July. The day had been very hot and it was very warm in the crowded chapel. Aunt Em's coat had stuck to the back of the varnished pew in which she was sitting with Mrs. Bassett, and when she stood up there was a loud, ripping noise. She leaned forward so that Mrs. Bassett could see if any damage had been done, but even when her sister-in-law, her lips suspiciously puckered, shook her head, Aunt Em was not convinced. She did not enjoy the singing because she thought that her coat must be torn. When she was home in South Lodge, she borrowed Uncle Percy's magnifying glass and examined the back of her coat to see that it was not marred by any loose threads or spots of varnish. Fortunately, no harm had been done.

'And that,' said Aunt Em, 'will be the very last time I go to Green Lane—even if it is my own niece who's singing there.'

Before the chapel had been built, in 1889, services had been held in people's homes in the winter, and on the common, under an oak tree, in summer-time. The congregation was made up of the blacksmith and the men who worked on the farms, and their wives and children. The weekly collections were small and it seemed that the dream of a chapel in Green Lane would never come true. Then a corn merchant in Chaxton died, and his widow, who had been born in Bretherton, bought the land and paid for the building of the chapel as a memorial to her husband. This year the anniversary was particularly important because twenty-five years had passed since the chapel had been built, and a special meeting was held in the schoolroom to discuss the plans for the celebration.

'I want the anniversary to be something that the children especially will always remember,' said Mr. Mitchell, the circuit minister. 'I propose that on the Saturday we take the children to Lyncombe for the day.'

'It's a long way from Bretherton to the sea,' said Mrs. Hawkins, doubtfully.

'But we can make an early start,' said Mr. Mitchell.

'I've lived for seventy years without seeing the sea,' said Mr. Blease, wistfully.

'Perhaps we can find room for some grown-ups, too,' said the minister, with a smile.

There was tremendous excitement among the chapel children at the prospect of going to the sea. The news went quickly round the village, and the children who went to the parish church were openly envious.

'You are lucky, Kate,' said Jessie Banks.

After a long discussion with the churchwardens, the vicar

announced to the choir boys and the pupils of the Sunday school that a visit to the seaside would be arranged later in the month.

'Copy-cats!' said the chapel children, scornfully.

The news reached Penrose Farm and South Lodge. Miss Nell allowed Kate to have the chosen Saturday as a holiday, and said that she need not return to the farm until Sunday evening, and on Friday Kate went home to the cottage where her brothers and sisters were in a state of bright-eyed excitement, which could not be dulled even by the unexpected arrival of Aunt Em, who had brought a bag of broad beans for Mrs. Bassett.

'A high old time you seem to be having out at Penrose Farm,' she said to Kate. 'A whole day's holiday and allowed to sleep home the night before as well! I don't know what things are coming to. It was never like that in my day, I can tell you. In my first place when I went out to work I was up at the crack of dawn and most nights I never got to bed till gone ten o'clock.'

'Have you ever been to the seaside, Aunt Em?' said Mary, hoping to divert her attention.

'No, I haven't,' said Aunt Em. 'And what's more, I can't say that I ever wanted to. Some of us are quite content with what we've got, but of course, it wouldn't do for us all to be the same, would it?'

She stayed until the younger children went to bed, and then opened her purse and placed two sixpences on the table.

'This is to spend tomorrow,' she said gruffly. 'Make sure you share it out between everybody fairly, Kate, and don't get spending it on lots of sticky sweets so that you'll be sick and make a nuisance of yourselves to everybody else.'

'Thank you, Aunt Em,' said Mary, hugging the ample form.

'Well now,' said Aunt Em, trying to hide her gratification, 'you're a good, deserving girl, Mary. I've always said that.'

Kate also stepped forward to kiss Aunt Em.

'I thought that you'd be too proud to kiss your old auntie,' said Aunt Em. 'I hope it keeps fine for you, I'm sure. Well,' she went on, glancing at the clock, 'this won't do, sitting around like this. Some of us have got work to do.'

Mrs. Bassett and Mary walked with her to the garden gate.

'Your lavender looks very well,' said Aunt Em. 'My bush isn't up to much this year. Percy must have moved it at the wrong time. I always like to have lavender in my linen cupboard.'

Mrs. Bassett said that when she picked the lavender she would save some for Aunt Em.

'Don't go robbing yourself,' said Aunt Em graciously. She walked slowly home to South Lodge, pleased that there was the promise of the lavender. She also wondered what had possessed her to be so generous with the two sixpences, and if there was any possibility of making Uncle Percy pay for her impulsive action.

It seemed strange to Kate to awaken the next morning in the small back bedroom with Mary by her side, and for a moment she thought that her mother would soon come in to say that it was time to get up or else she would be late for school. Then she realized what day it was, and she went quietly down the stairs to the kitchen where Mrs. Bassett was busy preparing sandwiches. Kate packed the food into two baskets and then went to call her brothers and sisters.

Breakfast was a noisy meal with everyone talking at once.

'There's a mist on the hills,' said Mary. 'It's going to be a lovely day.'

'Don't eat too much breakfast or we'll be late,' said Teddy, anxiously.

After the children had gone to the crossroads to await the carrier's waggonettes the cottage seemed very quiet indeed. Mr. Bassett did not come home at midday, and so Mrs. Bassett was going to spend the day baking bread and cakes for the anniversary tea.

As Mrs. Hawkins had said, it was a long way from Bretherton to the sea. In spite of the early start, the carriers did not expect to reach Lyncombe before twelve o'clock. The three waggonettes carried twenty-three excited children and six grown-ups. The Bassett children rode in the first waggonette with Mr. Mitchell and his wife and Mr. Blease. Mr. Mitchell was an excellent guide and pointed out various landmarks during the journey. There were so many things to see. After Chaxton cathedral there were the crossroads where once John Wesley had preached, and then Hilbury Castle with its portcullis and black swans on the moat. Men working in the fields waved as the waggonettes went by. They passed through a village where there was an old set of stocks by a market cross, and then they stopped at Canbury, which Mr. Mitchell said was famous for its china and lace, for a quarter of an hour. As they crossed the railway bridge at Canbury, a train went by, the first that they had ever seen.

'I counted seven carriages,' said Teddy.

As they neared the sea, gradually the countryside began to change. Instead of fields bounded by low stone walls, the road passed through moorland on which yellow gorse and purple-pink heather bloomed.

'Even the air's different,' said Mr. Blease.

'It's not much farther now,' said Mr. Mitchell. The waggonettes came slowly to the top of a hill and then he said softly, 'There it is.'

The Bassett children were silent as they looked down from the hill at the town of Lyncombe. In the haze the buildings were mistily pink and grey, and in the crescent-shaped bay the sea sparkled in the sunlight. The minister smiled as he glanced at the rapt expression on the children's faces. A tear ran down Mr. Blease's cheek, and Kate thought of Moses and the Promised Land. The waggonettes moved slowly down the hill into the town, past the tall terraced houses and the balconied hotels until they came to the sea-front. The smaller children were lifted down and they ran on to the beach while their elder brothers and sisters and the grown-ups came behind with the baskets. Teddy was the first to take off his boots and socks and he ran down to the water's edge closely followed by Mary, but Rose and the twins were rather overawed by the sea and

the green-topped cliffs, and they sat quietly by Kate, letting the sand run through their fingers while she unpacked the dinner basket.

'The water's lovely and warm,' said Teddy, when he and Mary came back for their dinner. There were several old-fashioned bathing machines drawn out into the sea, and men in striped bathing costumes could be seen swimming. Teddy would have liked to have been able to bathe, but no one from Bretherton possessed a bathing costume. The sandwiches which Mrs. Bassett had prepared tasted even more delicious in the open air, and all the food soon disappeared. Soon the twins were clamouring to go into the sea, and so Kate asked Mr. Blease to guard the baskets and boots and stockings. He sat smiling in the sun as he watched Kate, with a twin holding each hand, walk slowly down to the sea, while Teddy, Mary, and Rose ran on ahead. As Teddy had said, the water was quite warm, and so clear that they could see their toes on the sand.

In addition to her wages, Miss Nell had given Kate an extra shilling to spend, and with the shilling from Aunt Em and the money in the small purse which Mrs. Bassett had given her, there was more than enough to buy wooden spades for Rose and the twins and ice cream for them all from two of the stalls on the beach. In spite of the heat, Teddy went off on a beach-combing expedition organized by Mr. Mitchell, and the younger children were soon busy building sand-castles. Kate and Mary wanted to visit the shops, and Mrs. Hawkins readily agreed to keep an eye on Rose and the twins.

Mary was rather overawed by the large shops and bazaars and she was glad that Kate was there to lead the way. In one of the gift bazaars they bought a shaving mug for Mr. Bassett and a brooch shaped like a scallop shell for their mother. For Miss Nell there was a small, gilt-handled vase. There was also the question of a present for Aunt Em, and after a great deal of anxious consideration, they finally chose a red velvet pincushion set in a blue and white china high-heeled shoe.

It was very pleasant walking in the Lyncombe streets. It seemed to Kate that a seaside town had an atmosphere that could never be found anywhere else. It was not like the calm of Bretherton, or like Chaxton, with the bustle of the busy wharf and streets contrasting with the serenity of the cathedral close. In Lyncombe there seemed to be an air of gaiety and pleasure everywhere. The tall villas and hotels were newly painted and their gardens were bright with pink and blue hydrangeas. The white lace curtains at long wide windows were tied with bows of ribbon, the brass knockers shone, and the steps leading to the front doors were freshly whitened. From the lamp-posts hung baskets of flowers and ferns. The holiday atmosphere was matched by the people in the streets. The men wore straw hats, striped blazers, and white trousers, and the women and girls looked cool in pastel-coloured dresses. Small boys ran about, dressed in blue and white sailor suits. Kate thought that even the invalids in wheel-chairs seemed to be happy. When she looked in her purse she was surprised to find how much money had been spent, but she bought five sticks of pink rock and put them at the bottom of the rush basket. This was a secret shared only by Mary. The rock would be produced the next morning at home when the day by the sea was only a memory. They decided to walk along the whole length of the promenade, mingling with the fashionably dressed holiday-makers. Mary thought how nice it would be to have a frilled parasol like so many of the women carried. People sat contentedly on the beach and small figures ran to and from the water's edge. On the horizon they could see the grey outline of land, which Mr. Mitchell later told them was part of the mainland of Wales. At the far end of the promenade there was a wooden jetty where small fishing boats were moored. Two fishermen in dark blue jerseys were busy repairing lobster pots, and women in striped aprons stood behind stalls where mackerel, winkles, and cockles were for sale.

When the girls came back on to the beach, Rose and the twins were watching a Punch and Judy show, and Kate and Mary sat at the back of the audience with Mrs. Hawkins who whispered that the children had been as good as gold. Mr. Mitchell's beach-combing expedition arrived back in time for tea, and Teddy was very proud of his collection of seaweed, shells, driftwood, and pebbles. Promptly at half past four the waggonettes reappeared on the sea-front and there was an anxious five minutes for Kate when Teddy was unable to find his right boot. It was eventually discovered by Mary, half hidden by one of the twins' sand-castles.

'I never thought that there would be such a place,' said Mr.

Blease, when the waggonettes stopped at the top of the hill and they all had a last glimpse of the sea. 'It's worth coming I don't know how many miles for.'

Kate smiled in agreement. She knew that she would always remember the day that she first saw the sea.

There was not much talking in the first waggonette on the homeward journey. Everyone seemed to be silently storing up memories and impressions. As it grew dusk, May climbed on to Kate's lap and Mrs. Mitchell took Jimmy on her knee and soon the twins were asleep. The journey home seemed very long, but when they at last reached the crossroads at Bretherton, Mr. Bassett was waiting for them. As they were handed down from the waggonette the twins awoke, and refreshed by their sleep, they were able to walk home sturdily by their father's side, telling him of all they had seen at Lyncombe. When Mr. Bassett had come home from work, he was aware of how quiet it was and how empty the cottage seemed. It had been an unusually long and quiet day for Mrs. Bassett. After she had done all her housework and finished the baking for the anniversary tea, she had sat in the parlour with her sewing basket. When she heard the sound of the children's voices in the lane, she came to the door to meet them. As they ran to her smiling, there was no need for her to ask them if they had enjoyed themselves.

The presents from Lyncombe were a great success. Mr. Bassett used the shaving mug on Sunday morning and Mrs. Bassett wore the brooch to the anniversary service. As she stood alone on the platform to sing her solo, Mary could see it gleaming against the dark folds of her mother's blouse. Miss Nell cut a rose for the vase and placed it on her dressing-table.

'I don't expect you to go buying me presents,' said Aunt Em, 'and I'm sure I don't expect to be thanked for anything that I can manage to do for my brother's children, which is little enough, times and wages being what they are. All the same,' she added, 'I'm very much obliged to you.'

The pincushion was considered to be too fine for everyday use, and it was placed on the mantelpiece in the parlour of South Lodge.

Chapter 7

On Tuesday, the fourth of August, England and Germany were at war. At the service in the chapel in Green Lane on the following Sunday afternoon the minister and the congregation prayed for the safety of the country, and in a long sermon which Kate did not fully understand, Mr. Mitchell preached about David and Goliath and the Philistines. Then, after the collection had been taken and the two wooden alms dishes were placed on the communion table, Mr. Blease began to play the National Anthem on the old harmonium. As Kate sang with her arms held stiffly by her sides, she thought about the King and Queen in Buckingham Palace and wondered how they felt about their country being at war. When the service ended and the congregation came out into the hot summer afternoon, some of the men and women stood talking in small groups.

'I've got a lad that's been in the Army these two years,' said a thin, little woman. 'I didn't want him to go, but he was never a one to settle, and as soon as he was old enough he went off to enlist. Said he wanted to see foreign parts. Happen he will, now,' she sighed. 'Happen he'll see more than he bargained for.'

'I reckon it'll all be over by Christmas,' the wheelwright said. 'Our lads will soon put some salt on the old Kaiser's tail.'

'It doesn't seem right somehow—him being the old Queen's grandson. It's like family against family,' said Mrs. Hives, the dressmaker. 'Things would have been different if she'd still been alive. Still, times change, and I dare say that we'll see a lot more.'

The changes did not come about immediately, but the next time that Kate went into Chaxton there were enlistment posters on the pillars of the Corn Exchange where a room was being used as an army recruiting office, and as she went by, she saw several young men going in to enlist.

She found that the prospect of war made people react in differing ways. Aunt Em went into Chaxton and bought up as much

66

sugar, salt, and dried fruit as she could without arousing the suspicions of the shopkeepers. She told Mrs. Bassett that she felt in her bones that times were going to be hard, and it was up to everyone to look out for themselves.

'I've written to my daughter in Manchester,' said Mrs. Maslen, 'and told her that she had better come home. We might as well all be together at a time like this.' She held a flat-iron close to her cheek. 'I might as well have saved the ink and paper and stamp for all the good that it did,' she went on. 'She said that she was all right where she was and there was no cause for me to go worrying.'

One morning Kate was polishing the brass knocker on the front door when she heard the sound of footsteps on the gravel path, and she turned, thinking that it would be the postman, but instead of the blue uniformed figure of Mr. Bell, it was Sir Edward Carey who stood looking down at her. She was surprised and she felt her cheeks redden as she curtsied rather awkwardly, thinking of the old black apron she was wearing and of the polishing rag in her hand. Lady Margaret had spoken to her once during one of her weekly visits to the school, and she remembered how nervous and clumsy she had felt then, just as she did now. It was the gentry's way, she thought.

'Good morning,' said Sir Edward. 'I would like to see Miss Linden, if it's possible.'

'Yes, sir,' said Kate. 'She's upstairs.'

She opened the front door and waited for Sir Edward to go inside, but he stood in the path looking rather uncertainly at her.

'It's all right, sir,' she said quietly.

'Thank you,' said Sir Edward, and Kate hurried to open the door of the drawing-room. She was glad that she had been busy tidying the room earlier in the morning. The sun shone through the windows and gleamed on the brass fender and there was the faint scent of the lavender furniture polish she had used.

'I'll fetch Miss Nell, sir,' she said, and curtsied again. As she went upstairs she wondered if Miss Nell had ever been to Ellswood Park. Remembering the expression on Sir Edward's face, she thought that something very serious had happened. Miss Nell was just coming from the linen cupboard at the far end of the landing with some clean towels and she smiled inquiringly when she saw Kate.

'Yes, Kate,' she said. 'What is it?'

'Sir Edward Carey's here, Miss Nell,' said Kate.

'Here?' said Miss Nell. All the colour went from her face.

'He's in the drawing-room,' said Kate uncertainly.

'All right,' said Miss Nell, and she hurried along the landing. Kate followed behind her. When they reached the top of the stairs she saw that Sir Edward had come out of the drawing-room and now stood in the hall looking up at them.

'I had to come, Nell,' he said. 'My enlistment papers are through.'

Miss Nell ran down the stairs, not seeming to care that she had dropped the towels. Kate stepped back on to the landing so that she could not see Sir Edward and Miss Nell and waited until she heard the sound of the drawing-room door being closed. She picked up the towels that Miss Nell had dropped and went into the bedrooms, taking the used towels from the rails of the wash-stands and putting the fresh ones in their place. She was glad to be able to do something to help Miss Nell. In her own room she glanced at the clock on the dressing-table. It was twenty minutes past eleven. The Master would come back for his dinner at twelve o'clock. She went back downstairs into the kitchen and the plates on the dresser and the iron saucepans boiling on the range seemed somehow reassuring. She sat looking at the clock, afraid that the Master would come back before Sir Edward had gone, but at five and twenty minutes to twelve Miss Nell came into the kitchen. She went to the range and began lifting the lids of the saucepans.

'Sir Edward came to say that he is going away to the war,' she said after a little while.

Kate thought desperately for something to say to comfort her.

'People were saying at the chapel that they think that it will all be over by Christmas,' she said.

'I hope they're right, Kate,' said Miss Nell.

As Kate began to lay the table in the dining-room, she thought of Miss Grace's happiness on her wedding day, and she wondered if Miss Nell and Sir Edward would be married when the war was over.

'Sir Edward's off to France tomorrow,' said Aunt Em, when she arrived the next Sunday afternoon at the Bassetts' cottage. 'You can always rely on the gentry to do the right thing. And not only the gentry either,' she added. She went on to say that the

68

husband of Uncle Percy's sister Maude who lived at Ditton had been called up because he, too, was a member of the Territorial Army.

'And that is it,' said Aunt Em. 'It means if anything goes wrong, the men in the Territorials are the first to go. Maude won't be able to stay in the cottage because the farmer will want it for the new man who's coming to take her husband's place.'

'What is she going to do, then?' asked Mrs. Bassett.

'Well, she can stay there until the end of the month,' said Aunt Em, 'and then she'll just have to go. She can't find another cottage to rent, so she's going back to live with her mother. You know how small her place is. There's only two bedrooms there. I don't know how they're going to manage. There'll be no room for the furniture, so she's trying to get it stored in one of the barns at the farm. There's four children to think about. The eldest is only seven.'

As Kate listened to Aunt Em she realized that it must be an anxious time for many people.

'And there's another thing,' said Aunt Em. 'The allowance the Government pays a soldier's wife isn't very much, not when you really think about it. When Maude's husband was working on the farm, they didn't have to pay any rent for the cottage and there was always a free quart of milk each day and as much firewood as they wanted. He had a big allotment where he grew all his own potatoes and corn, which was a big saving. Maude's going to miss all that. It's bad enough worrying all the time because your man's gone to the war, without having to wonder how you're going to keep a roof over your head and make ends meet every week.'

Kate knew that the days which followed were full of anxiety for Miss Nell. In the evenings after the Master had finished reading the newspaper, she would bring it out into the kitchen and sit reading it with an old atlas open on the table beside her. Once the Master came into the kitchen for a box of matches for his pipe, and Miss Nell quickly placed the newspaper on top of the atlas so that he could not see the map of France at which she had been looking. After supper Kate would read the newspaper too, and try to find on the map the names of the French and Belgian towns where all the fighting was taking place. Then letters with foreign stamps on the envelopes began to arrive at the farm. The postman usually called at about half past eleven, when the Master was out at work either in the yard or in the fields, and so only Kate saw the happiness which they gave to Miss Nell.

At the farm the men were busy with the harvest, and as they were working late while the fine weather lasted, Miss Nell took beer in the stone jars in wicker baskets out to them in the fields. The corn was cut by a horse-drawn reaping machine and the men came behind and set up the sheaves to dry in bundles of six and seven and Kate immediately thought of the circle of stones on the downs by Ringstone Farm. Whenever she saw a field of corn waving in the summer breeze she thought how restless it seemed, almost as if it wanted to break out of the restraining hedges or spill over the low stone boundary walls, but once the corn was cut and piled in stooks on the coarse stubble it seemed like groups of old people sitting contentedly in the sun. Kate picked a handful of poppies from the hedge to place in the vase on the dresser in the kitchen. Tom Collier waved out to her as he went by driving one of the big red and blue painted waggons drawn by one of the grey carthorses.

The Master owned one of the very few threshing machines in the district, and corn from the outlying farms was brought to be threshed in the largest barn at Penrose Farm. Most of the villagers rented allotments on which they grew potatoes and corn, and their grain was also brought to the farm for threshing. When all the corn at Penrose Farm had been cut, the Master allowed the wives and children of his men to go into the fields to collect any ears of corn which lay among the stubble. The village people called this leazing. Of all the work that Kate did at home, leazing was the one task which she hated most of all. Mr. Bassett rented a large allotment and on a quarter of an acre he grew his own corn. Mrs. Bassett always baked her own bread, and ever since Kate could remember, a large, white sack of flour had stood in one corner of the kitchen at home. The sun never seemed to be so hot as it did on the day that Mrs. Bassett would say that it was leazing time. Kate's back ached and her hands were sore from the prickles and the sharp stalks of the stubble. She thought that the small bundles of corn which she and her mother harvested did not really compensate for all the discomfort, but she knew that nothing was to be wasted.

When the plums were ripe, Tom Collier spent an afternoon in the orchard filling deep bushel baskets with the dusky red fruit, and the next day Miss Nell was busy making jam. There was a basket of plums to be taken to the kitchen at Ellswood Park, because Mrs. Bingham, the cook, always said that there were no plums as fine as those from Penrose Farm for jam-making.

'I sent a message by one of the maids last Sunday,' said Miss Nell, 'and told her to expect the fruit this week. Tom will drive the trap, and perhaps you'd like to go as well, Kate. It will make a little outing.'

Kate was ready at half past two and stood by the back door, waiting for Tom to appear. 'I think we'll go into the park by North Lodge,' he said, 'it will be the nearest.'

Kate was glad that Aunt Em would not have to open the lodge gates for them. She was looking forward to seeing Ellswood Park. When they reached North Lodge, Mrs. Croucher came hurrying out to open the gates for them. She was a thin, rather harassed-looking woman, but she gave them a bright smile as the trap went by. The drive was bounded on each side by black iron railings, and stretched away in the distance like a white ribbon between the wide, green parklands. They had not gone very far when one of the gamekeepers appeared and he put up his hand for Tom to stop.

'And where might you be going?' he asked.

'Taking these plums up to Mrs. Bingham at the Park,' said Tom, easily.

'Right, then,' said the gamekeeper. 'Go round to the back door, mind. Take the turning on the left.'

'As if we'd do anything else,' Tom said to Kate, as they drove off. 'Can you see us walking up to the front door and ringing the bell as if we were gentry?'

After they had driven for about a mile and a half, the house came into view, and Kate could see tall gables, dark latticed windows, and twisting chimneys. Terraced gardens sloped towards a lake.

'It's a nice place,' said Tom.

'It's beautiful,' said Kate.

They drove under a stone archway and came into a cobbled yard where there was a square clock tower with a black and gold clock. In the stables, two grooms were busy with the horses. The arrival of the trap had been seen by Mrs. Bingham from her kitchen window and she came out into the yard. She was a short, grey-haired woman, wearing small gold ear-rings and a grey print dress.

'It's Kate Bassett, isn't it?' she said. 'I remember your aunt, Mrs. Potter at South Lodge, telling me about you.' She took a plum from the basket. 'The plums are as good as ever, I see,' she said. 'I don't know what you get up to at Penrose Farm, but these plums are certainly the best I've ever tasted. In my opinion, Ellswood plums are never up to much, and I don't care who hears me say it. Come on inside,' she went on, as Tom and Kate lifted the basket down from the trap, and they followed her through a long corridor until they came to the kitchen, which seemed to Kate to be almost as big as the chapel. The floor was of orange and black tiles and the white walls gleamed with an array of copper moulds. There were two huge kitchen ranges and a large dresser with pink and white crockery. Two maids were busy preparing afternoon tea. One was pouring cream into a silver jug and the other arranged tiny sandwiches and cakes on silver dishes. By the kitchen sink, a young girl of Kate's age was peeling potatoes.

'Right, then,' said Mrs. Bingham, 'you can put your basket under the table.'

She took an envelope from the drawer of the white, scrubbed kitchen table. 'And you can give that to Miss Linden.'

She spoke to the girl at the sink.

'Two glasses of barley water, Maggie,' she said, 'and peel those potatoes thinner. You'll have us all in the workhouse at that rate.'

She smiled, pleased at her own joke, and Maggie blushed and hurried into the pantry and reappeared with a blue and white pitcher. While Tom and Kate drank their barley water, Mrs. Bingham and Maggie emptied the basket, putting the plums into three big, earthenware bowls. Watching Maggie, Kate realized that if Aunt Em had had her way, she would have been one of the kitchen-maids at Ellswood Park. Perhaps she would have filled glasses with barley water for Tom and a girl from Penrose Farm. The thought was not unpleasant, but she was glad that she worked for Miss Nell.

Just as she and Tom were leaving, two footmen in blue livery came into the kitchen with trays and carried away the silver tea service and the tiny cakes and sandwiches.

'Lady Margaret's tea,' explained Mrs. Bingham. 'Thank Miss Linden for the plums. Mind how you go.'

'How would you like to have your tea out of a silver teapot?' asked Tom, as they drove home.

'I don't suppose that it would taste any better than it does from my little, yellow one,' replied Kate, with a laugh, but she thought about Miss Nell and Sir Edward, and she wondered if there would ever come a time when the footmen would carry the silver tea service to Miss Nell in the drawing-room of Ellswood Park.

Chaxton Flower Show was to be held on the second Saturday in September and Miss Nell said that if Kate would like to go she could finish work immediately after dinner on the Saturday afternoon. Kate arranged to take her brothers and sisters, none of whom had ever been to the Flower Show before. One of the farm men was taking a load of newly threshed grain to the mill at Chaxton, setting out at one o'clock, and Miss Nell said that they could all have a ride on the back of the cart.

'There will be plenty of room,' she said, and when she paid Kate her wages, she also gave her an extra shilling to spend at the Show. After the dinner things had been washed up, Kate changed into her brown dress and put on her straw hat, while Miss Nell packed her tea into a small wicker basket.

'Enjoy yourself,' she said, smiling as Kate went out through the side gate to wait in the lane for Fred Chivers and the cart.

Fred Chivers was well known for his punctuality on the farm. 'As regular as old Fred Chivers,' was one of the Master's sayings. Miss Nell glanced at her watch when she heard the sound of the horse and cart in the lane. It was exactly one o'clock.

'Good afternoon, maid,' said Fred to Kate. 'Out to see the day's sights at Chaxton, then?'

'Yes,' said Kate, as she climbed up on to the cart and sat beside him.

'You've got company, too,' said Fred, as Tom Collier came running down the lane and sat on one of the sacks of grain, grinning at Kate. Mrs. Bassett and all Kate's brothers and sisters were waiting at the gate by the cottage, and they began to wave as soon as the cart came round the bend in the lane. They were all wearing big, wide-brimmed hats to shelter them from the sun, and the girls were wearing their best white pinafores. Kate was surprised when Tom Collier jumped down from the cart and

began to lift the smaller children up on to the sacks, while Teddy and Mary scrambled up by themselves.

'Have a good time, then,' said Mrs. Bassett, as she gave Kate a small amount of spending money for the children and the old rush basket which contained their tea, 'and mind,' she said to the little ones, 'that you're good children and do as Kate says.'

Kate sat with May on her lap and Jimmy squeezed in beside her and Fred Chivers, who obligingly moved along in his seat.

'Reckon as how we can make room for a little 'un,' he said.

Rose, Mary, and Teddy perched themselves upon the sacks at the back of the cart with Tom. Teddy especially seemed to get on particularly well with Tom, who produced a piece of string from his pocket and began to teach Teddy the intricacies of knot tying. As they drew near to Chaxton, their progress was made slower by the number of carts and traps which they met on the roads. Everyone, it seemed, was going to the Flower Show.

'There's the spire of the cathedral,' said Fred, and Kate again

experienced the feeling of pleasure and wonder which she felt every time she saw it.

As they drove into the town Fred said, 'I'll set you down by the Corn Exchange steps, and then I'm on to the mill with the Master's corn. Be here at six o'clock, mind.'

'Thank you, Mr. Chivers,' said Kate, as the children began to clamber down from the waggon.

'And you be careful, young Tom,' said Fred. 'Don't get trying to enlist or any such foolishness.'

Kate thought that Tom would go off by himself, but instead, he just stood there on the steps of the Corn Exchange, smiling uncertainly. In the end, Teddy settled everything by saying, 'I'll walk with you, Tom,' and so they all went into the Corn Exchange together. In honour of the occasion, someone had placed a wreath of real flowers round the brow of the statue at the top of the steps. All the exhibits were displayed on long trestle tables in the main hall.

'Best Show we've ever had,' said a red-faced man wearing a big rosette, denoting that he was one of the judges at the Show, 'war or no war.'

There certainly was a great variety of fruit and vegetables, and Kate thought that she had never seen such long runner beans, such huge potatoes, beetroot, and marrows. Apples and pears had been arranged in pyramids, and flowers, in great splashes of colour, red, blue, yellow, orange, and white, filled the high-ceilinged room with the scent of late summer. In the house-keeping section there were cakes arranged on high glass stands, pots of jam and pickles, and bowls of eggs. Kate thought that Miss Nell's gooseberry jam was a far better colour than the pot which had been awarded first prize. Miss Nell would easily have won if she had entered. Kate would have liked to have stayed longer and have seen the sewing and embroidery, but as soon as the organs at the fairground began playing, the twins grew rest-less. As they came out of the Corn Exchange, there was a woman walking up and down the steps, carrying a board on a pole on which a big white card had been fixed.

'Votes for women,' said Tom, looking at the card. 'I wonder what she's doing that for?'

'Oh, come on,' said Teddy. 'Let's go on into the fair. We don't want to bother about any old votes.'

Kate remembered that once Miss Grace and Miss Nell had discussed having the vote after reading something in the paper. 'I think we'd make as good a job as the men,' Miss Grace had said. 'One day there might be women Members of Parliament.'

There was already a large crowd of people at the fairground. Kate said they would first of all look at everything, and then decide how to spend their money. The twins liked the round-abouts with carved galloping horses to ride upon. They were painted yellow and outlined in red and blue, and as the round-abouts revolved, the horses moved up and down on poles of twisted brass. Teddy wanted to go on the swinging boats which were painted black and white and were pulled by green and red plush-handled ropes. Although she was just a little afraid of the brown-faced woman with gold rings in her ears who stood behind the stall, Rose gazed longingly at the golden brown toffee apples. She caught hold of Mary's reassuring hand, and even managed to smile back at the brown-faced woman. Mary looked

at a pile of sunbonnets and hats and decided that when she left
school and went out to work, the very first thing that she would
buy from her wages would be a blue and white gingham sunbonnet. At the boxing booth Tom stared respectfully at a man in
a red silk cloak who stood on the platform and stared contemp-
tuously at the crowd, while a much smaller man beat on a drum
and called for volunteers to challenge the champion of six

counties. Kate stood for a long time at one of the china stalls,
admiring a tea service in pink and white.

'Let's go on the swinging boats,' said Teddy, so they all
crowded into two boats, with Kate and Mary pulling the ropes
of one and Tom and Teddy pulling the other, seeing which of the
boats would go higher. Mary said that she thought she and Kate
were the winners, but Kate had a suspicion that Tom had
deliberately allowed them to win. Then they went on the round-
abouts with Kate holding May and Tom holding Jimmy, all of

them screaming and laughing so much that they felt quite out of breath when the ride ended. Kate said that the next thing they must do was to buy a present for their parents, and after spending a long time at the stalls considering the merits of all the goods displayed, they bought a pair of bootlaces for their father and a small cream jug for Mrs. Bassett. Tom chose the same for his parents. At quarter to four an army brass band arrived and began to play a series of military marches. All the men looked very smart in their uniforms of scarlet and blue. A special platform had been built for them and Kate thought how hot they must be sitting up there, with the sun shining on the brass instruments. When the first piece of music ended, everyone clapped and cheered, and when the conductor turned round to acknowledge the applause with a stiff bow, Kate thought that he looked just like the man on one of the enlistment posters on the pillars of the Corn Exchange. After Teddy had said three times that he was hungry, Kate thought that it must be time to have tea, so they went to the far edge of the fairground and sat down under the hedge. She began to unpack the rush basket, and then she realized that Tom had disappeared. She felt rather disappointed that he had gone off without saying anything at all. He had helped her with the children all the afternoon, and she had not even thanked him properly. She knew that not every lad of fifteen would have spent so much time carrying May or Jimmy when they were tired. Then the next time that she looked up she saw him coming towards her, bringing two bottles of ginger beer and a bag of currant buns.

'I had to go and get my tea,' he said, sitting down on the grass beside Teddy.

Mrs. Bassett had packed bread and butter and slices of seed cake in the rush basket, together with a big bottle of cold tea and a tin mug. When Kate unpacked Miss Nell's wicker basket there were twelve cheese sandwiches and the fruit cake which she had baked the previous afternoon, and which Kate had thought to be Miss Nell's usual weekly cake-making. She had also put in a small knife wrapped in tissue paper, and a bottle of lemonade. Oh, Miss Nell, thought Kate, you are good. I wish you were here with us.

They all sat round in a circle with all the food in the middle, laughing and talking, eating and drinking, until everything had disappeared except the bottles, the tin mug, and Miss Nell's knife. Mary took the young children off to see if they could find a few flowers to take home, while Tom just lay back in the grass with his cap over his eyes. Kate looked at the broad-shouldered figure in the corduroy suit and heavy boots and she thought of the number of times that she had seen Miss Crompton bring her cane down on Tom's back, so hard that sometimes a cloud of dust arose from his jacket. Tom had often been late for school, and Miss Crompton always punished unpunctuality by caning. If she had known that Tom's father was a very strict man who expected Tom to do a certain amount of work at home each day before he set out on the three-mile journey to school, she might possibly have been more lenient when she saw Tom trying to come into the classroom unnoticed while the rest of the school were singing the opening hymn.

When the children came back, they all went for a last look round the fair and had one more ride on the swinging boats. This time their ride was much longer than before, because most of the people were having their tea, and the showman was wise enough to see that two boats going to and fro in the air with two groups of children laughing and shouting were a far better advertisement than the same two boats lying still and empty. When the ride came to an end, Tom asked a man with a pocket watch what time it was. It was five minutes to six. Tom carried Jimmy, Kate carried May, and with Rose, Teddy and Mary hurrying as fast as they could, they made their way to the Corn Exchange. Most of the people they met were going back to the fairground and so their progress was slow. When they reached the Corn Exchange the cart was not there. The hands of the clock on the clock tower showed that it was quarter past six, and Kate's heart sank when she thought of the long walk back to Chaxton.

'Oh, Tom,' she said with a quiver in her voice which she could not control. 'I thought that Mr. Chivers would have waited.'

'So did I,' said Tom. He looked at Kate and saw the sadness in her face. 'In fact, I know that he would. Tell you what, I'll go down to the mill and see if he's there. Something must have happened.'

Kate and the children watched him as he walked down the street, and when he was out of sight, they sat down on the steps of the Corn Exchange. May began to cry and Kate rocked her in her arms, trying to comfort her. It seemed such a sad ending to what

79

had been a lovely day. There was just the faint hope that perhaps Mr. Chivers had been delayed at the mill, but she remembered that he was well known for his punctuality. She wondered what her mother would think when she saw the cart go by the cottage, and Miss Nell would be cross because she would be late getting back to the farm.

'There they are,' shouted Teddy, beginning to jump up and down with excitement, and Kate looked up and saw Tom and Fred Chivers coming along by the clock tower.

'Sorry I'm late, maid,' said Fred Chivers, as they all climbed thankfully up on to the cart. 'They had a bit of trouble with one of the grinders at the mill, and it put them a bit behind with the work. Had a good day?' he said to Teddy.

'Yes,' Teddy replied, 'the best day ever.'

Kate sat in the front with May, while the others sat in the back of the cart. May was soon asleep, and several times on the slow, homeward journey, Mr. Chivers glanced sideways at Kate as she sat with her arms round the sleeping child. There was a kind expression in his usually sharp eyes. May did not wake up even when the cart stopped at the cottage and Mrs. Bassett took her from Kate and carried her indoors.

'Don't forget the presents,' Kate whispered to Mary, as she handed her the rush basket, and Mary nodded, pleased to be the one chosen to make the presentation.

'Good-bye, Tom,' said Teddy, 'and thank you, Mr. Chivers.'

'That's all right, lad,' said Fred, and he drove the cart the rest of the way back to the farm in silence. When they reached the side gate, Kate jumped down from the cart and was surprised to find how stiff her arms felt.

'Good night, Mr. Chivers,' she said. 'Thank you very much.'

'Good night, maid,' said Fred, gruffly.

'Good night, Tom,' Kate said to the figure stretched out on the sacks in the back of the cart. 'It's been a lovely day.'

'Good night,' replied Tom. He lay with his cap over his eyes.

As they drove on down to the farmyard, Fred said, 'That Kate Bassett, now, she's what I call a smartish girl.'

Chapter 8

'I saw three gipsy caravans when I was coming along Ashton Lane,' said Mrs. Maslen, one Monday morning. 'Going to the common, I shouldn't wonder. Dirty thieving things. They'll steal anything, they will. They'd have the clothes off your back if they had half a chance. With them about, we'll have to make sure that everything's locked up at night.'

'I expect they'll be round the houses before the week is out,' said Miss Nell.

'Well, we could do with some more clothes-pegs,' said Mrs. Maslen grudgingly. 'I can't think why anybody would want to live in a caravan with everyone crowded into a little space like sheep in a pen. It doesn't seem right, somehow.'

Kate was glad that she was not a gipsy girl. The caravans which suddenly appeared on the common at regular intervals throughout the year were small and shabby. The men looked slyly from under bushy eyebrows and they spoke to their wives and children in a strange form of dialect, and sometimes they used a secret sign language. Once, as the Dassett children passed the gipsies' camp on their way to school, one of the women had been cooking something in an iron pot hanging from three sticks over a smoking fire. Everyone knew that the gipsies were a strange people. They even had their own queen. One of the girls at school said that her grandmother had told her that gipsies liked to eat hedgehogs, and that when gipsies were married, instead of going to the church or chapel as everyone else did, they just jumped over a broomstick. When a gipsy died, the caravan in which he had lived was burned.

Kate had once read a story in one of Miss Crompton's books about a princess who had been stolen by gipsies, and after many adventures she had been rescued by a woodcutter who was really a prince from a neighbouring country in disguise. None of the gipsy children that she had seen ever looked as if they were perhaps a prince or princess, and Kate was certain that the idea of gipsies stealing children was just another story. However, she was always glad when they had passed the common if the gipsies were there, and even Teddy, who declared that he wasn't afraid of anything, always quickened his step until they were safely past.

The Bassett children often played in the fields and woods and knew where the best blackberries, crab-apples, and hazel-nuts could be found. Kate and Mary had made a collection of wild flowers and Mrs. Bassett had allowed Kate to press them in the big family Bible which had belonged to her own mother and which had been printed in 1805. It was illustrated with rather strange pictures. There was a picture of Pharaoh's daughter finding Moses in the bulrushes. She wore a crown on her head and a full-skirted dress so that she looked more like an English queen than an Egyptian princess. There was also a picture of Samson bearing away the gates of Gaza on his shoulders, wearing a long robe and a broad-brimmed hat. On the front inside cover of the Bible were the names of Mrs. Bassett's brothers and sisters and also her own name, and below them were the names of her own children.

One flower which Kate and Mary had so far been unable to find was a wild daffodil and it was rather annoying to see the gipsy women going to each house in the village in spring-time with baskets bright with the yellow flowers. Kate thought that the only way in which they would ever discover where the wild daffodils grew would be to follow the caravans, but she did not think that she would ever summon up enough courage to do so. She would also have liked to have been able to discover where the gipsies found the mistletoe at Christmas-time. The Bassetts had their own holly tree in the back garden, but Mrs. Bassett always bought some mistletoe from the gipsies whose carts were piled high with the white-berried branches. Mr. Bassett had placed a few of the berries beneath the bark of one of the apple trees and the children had waited hopefully for any signs of the pale green leaves to appear, but even after three attempts, the pearl-like berries refused to germinate.

'It looks as if we shall have to rely upon the gipsies after all,' said Mrs. Bassett with a smile.

'I can't think for the life of me why you want to go cluttering up your best apple tree with stuff you only want at Christmas-time,' said Aunt Em. 'After all, it's only an old plant when all is said and done.'

To the Bassetts, however, mistletoe was as much a part of Christmas as were holly and carols.

Kate and Miss Nell were in the kitchen preparing vegetables when Mrs. Maslen came in from the scullery later in the morning and said that one of the gipsy women was outside with a basket of clothes-pegs.

'I told her to stay where she is and not move a step, Miss Nell,' said Mrs. Maslen. 'I know what they can be like. I'd best come with you,' she added, as Miss Nell took her purse from the dresser. 'I've got my boiler stick ready.'

Miss Nell glanced at Kate and there was a little smile on her lips as she went out with Mrs. Maslen, and then Kate could hear the soft, wheedling voice of the gipsy. She had just finished peeling the potatoes when Miss Nell came back with the clothes-pegs. Kate glanced at her and thought that there was rather a serious expression on her face.

'Is anything wrong, Miss Nell?' she asked.

'No,' said Miss Nell with a smile. 'Our gipsy says that she can tell fortunes, too, Kate. Off you go and see what lies in store for you.'

Kate went out to the scullery door where Mrs. Maslen stood with the boiler stick in her hand, watching the gipsy. She had just had her fortune told and she seemed in a good humour.

'And this is the little lady, is it?' said the gipsy in a husky voice. 'Will you cross my hand with silver?'

'There's no need for that,' said Mrs. Maslen. 'Miss Nell's given you more than enough already.'

'Give me your hand, then, child,' said the gipsy. She was an old woman and Kate wondered if she had walked all the way from the common. Her skin was very brown and wrinkled and her eyes were very black, but her teeth were as strong and white as those of a much younger woman. She wore a brown cloak and skirt and her hair was hidden by a red and white handkerchief.

'Not frightened of the future, are you, maid?' said the old woman.

'No,' said Kate, giving her hand to the gipsy, who stared intently into it as if she was reading a book. Mrs. Maslen moved closer, an expectant smile on her face.

83

'I see a long life for you, my dear,' said the gipsy, after a little while. 'I can see you in a big town far away from here, and that's where you'll meet someone who'll be very dear to you. I can see you as an old lady with children and grandchildren round you, but that's not yet, not for a long time.'

She smiled at Kate and said, 'Disappointed, maid? Most folk want to be told that they'll be rich and drive in a fine carriage. Well, I dare say that some people will, but it's not for you. It'll be a hard life, but it will be a long one, and a good one, unless I'm very much mistaken.'

'Thank you,' said Kate, but she was rather disappointed. She had not really expected to be told that one day she would be rich and wear silk dresses and jewellery, but it seemed to her that what the gipsy had foretold seemed rather ordinary and dull.

'You've got a lucky face,' said the gipsy. 'You've got a cup of milk for a poor old gipsy woman, haven't you?'

'No,' said Mrs. Maslen firmly, pointing to the gate. 'You've had your money for the clothes-pegs and you've been well paid for the fortune-telling, so now be off with you.' She opened the side gate and watched as the gipsy picked up her basket and walked slowly down the path and out into the lane.

'Always trying to get something for nothing, those gipsies,' said Mrs. Maslen as she shut the gate. 'Still, fortune-telling makes for a bit of fun, if nothing else. Do you know what she told me, Kate? She said that I was going to have a young lady visitor soon. That could very well be my girl from up in Manchester. It would certainly do my eyes good to see her again after such a long time.'

'Did Miss Nell have her fortune told?' asked Kate.

'Of course she did. Miss Nell was always a one for a bit of fun. It didn't seem much of a fortune, though,' went on Mrs. Maslen with a thoughtful expression on her face. 'The gipsy said something about there being someone across the water who was very dear to her, and that between two harvests there would be a great many changes made. I don't know what she meant by that, I'm sure.'

Kate thought of Sir Edward away in France.

'Do you really believe that people can foretell the future, Mrs. Maslen?' she asked.

'I don't know,' said the washerwoman. 'I'm not saying that I do, and then again, I'm not saying that I don't. Perhaps I will if I get a letter to say my daughter's coming home for a bit. Still, this won't get the wash done, will it? I must get on, I suppose. It looks as if it's going to be a good day for drying clothes.'

Miss Nell was busy rolling pastry when Kate went back into the kitchen.

'Well, Kate,' she said, 'and what did the gipsy promise you—a handsome husband and a thousand pounds a year?'

When Kate told her what the gipsy had said, Miss Nell smiled. 'I think you're going to be the luckiest of us all. All that she'd promise me was that there would be some changes made.'

That evening Mr. Linden and Miss Nell had been invited to a whist drive given by the parents of Miss Grace's husband and Miss Nell had arranged that Mrs. Bray should come to the farm house to spend the evening with Kate.

'She'll be here about half past seven,' said Miss Nell. 'See that she has a good supper, Kate. We shall be back at about ten o'clock.'

After the Master and Miss Nell had driven away in the trap, Kate went into the drawing-room for one of Miss Nell's books. There was still half an hour before Mrs. Bray was due to arrive, and once she was there Kate knew that there would be no further opportunity to read. One of the books Miss Nell had suggested that she might like was *Cranford*, and Kate was sitting in the kitchen laughing over the story when she heard Mrs. Bray knock at the back door. She went along the passage and opened the door but, instead of the comfortable figure of Mrs. Bray, a man was standing there, his eyes glittering against the swarthiness of his skin.

'Hello, missy. Anyone about?' he said in a gruff voice.

'No,' said Kate sharply.

She slammed the door and managed to shoot the middle bolt across, in spite of the trembling of her hands. She was fairly certain that the man was one of the gipsies, and she remembered what Mrs. Maslen had said about them stealing things. She ran into all the downstairs rooms and made certain that all the windows were fastened and the doors locked and bolted. She was aware of how quiet it was in the house and as she came into the hall the ticking of the clock seemed unnaturally loud. She moved on tiptoe along the passage and stood by the back door. There was no sound outside and for a moment she thought that the man had gone and then, as she waited, she saw that the knob of the door was slowly being turned. She had polished the brass knob every day that she had been at Penrose Farm but instead of an ordinary everyday object it now gleamed mysteriously. Hardly daring to breathe, she carried a chair from the kitchen and, standing on it, she was able to reach up and push the heavy bolt on the top of the door into position. Unless the man broke one of the windows, she was quite safe. She thought of Mrs. Maslen's boiler stick, but the door that led into the scullery was bolted. Then she remembered the big, brass-handled poker in the drawing-room, and she found that just to hold it in her hand gave her a sense of security. She listened intently, hoping that she would hear the gipsy's footsteps going away in the distance, but everything was still and silent. The brass door knob still gleamed in the half light of the passage and it seemed to Kate to have the same fascination as that of the bright red berries of the belladonna bushes which hung in the hedges like clusters of glass beads. She went to the kitchen window and looked out, but she could not see the back door from there. Then she wondered if the gipsy had gone to the farmyard and she ran upstairs to her own room and looked out across the field. She could not see anyone moving about and the farm buildings had a quiet, reassuring air, so she came back downstairs and listened again at the back door. She could hear nothing, and then, after what seemed a long time, there was some more knocking. The knocking was repeated, but Kate remained quite still with the poker in her hand. Then she heard Mrs. Bray's voice calling 'Kate, are you there, Kate?' and relief seemed to flood through her whole being, making her feel so giddy that she could hardly keep her balance as she stood on the chair to reach up to the top bolt.

Mrs. Bray heard the sound of the bolt being drawn back. 'All bolted and barred up already then, maid?' she said with a smile when Kate at last opened the door. Then she saw the poker lying on the floor and she looked intently at Kate.

'Are you all right, Kate?' she said sharply. 'What's happened?'

'It was a gipsy, a man,' said Kate. 'He came to the back door.'

'I saw a man in the lane,' said Mrs. Bray. 'I didn't take much notice of him because I was late setting out. My sister called on me, and didn't leave until half past six. I was all behind with the washing-up.' She put her arm round Kate.

'You've had a bit of a shock, Kate, but it's all right now. Let me make you a cup of tea.'

While they waited for the kettle to boil, the clock in the hall struck eight. Kate was surprised. She thought that she must have stood in the passage for several hours until she heard the sound of Mrs. Bray's voice.

The rest of the evening was spent with Kate listening to Mrs. Bray who sat knitting and talking of her childhood in North Devon. She had once lived in a small fishing village and remembering how much she had enjoyed her day at Lyncombe, Kate thought how wonderful it must be to live by the sea. It had been arranged that the Master would drive Mrs. Bray home, and when she heard the sound of Ladybird and the trap outside, she rose and put on her coat and hat. She had a quick word with Miss Nell before climbing up into the trap, and then Miss Nell came into the kitchen with a serious look on her face, but she seemed relieved when Kate said that everything was all right.

'He didn't get into the house, Miss Nell,' she said, 'but I don't know if he went down to the farmyard.'

'That can wait until tomorrow morning,' said Miss Nell.

Kate went to bed soon afterwards, and before Miss Nell went to her own room, she listened outside Kate's door and went away quietly after she was satisfied that she was asleep. Kate had a strange dream that she would have had difficulty in explaining to anyone the next morning. She dreamed that she had been walking on the common and a big gipsy man jumped up from behind a blackberry bush and took her to an encampment of caravans where the gipsy queen sat on a golden throne beneath an oak tree. She was wearing a necklace and bracelets of pearls, but when the man made Kate kneel before the throne she could see that the queen's jewels were really mistletoe berries, and she had laughed in surprise, remembering the necklaces she and Mary used to make from rosehips. As she laughed, the gipsy camp disappeared and she was alone, walking on the common, and then she opened her eyes to the reassuring half light of her own attic room. When she came downstairs to begin the day's work, the only thing to remind her of the previous evening was the brass-handled poker lying on the dresser.

Mrs. Maslen was not in a very good humour when she arrived at eight o'clock.

'I see that the gipsies have left the common,' she said. 'And a good riddance to bad rubbish. I don't believe they can tell your fortune, either. You remember what that old clothes-peg seller told me—that I was going to have a young lady visitor? I thought that it was going to be my daughter from Manchester. I had a visitor right enough. My daughter-in-law. She wanted to borrow my sewing machine, if you please. Had some notion about making some blouses. Fine blouses they'd have turned out to be. No one touches that machine except me, I told her, but she kept pestering me, and in the finish it ended up with me cutting out the material myself and promising that I'd make it up for her as well.'

The Master and the men made a thorough search of the garden and the farm buildings, but everything was in its place and nothing appeared to have been stolen.

'I'm sorry that you had that fright, Kate,' said Miss Nell.

When she went home on Sunday afternoon, Kate told her mother what had happened at the farm while they were alone in the kitchen preparing the tea. Remembering her own fear, she did not want to frighten the younger children. Aunt Em eventually found out about the gipsy's visit from the wife of one of the farm men, and she told Mrs. Bassett that she kept the brass-tipped walking-stick that had belonged to her father by the back door in case of any unwelcome visitors.

'Not of course, that any gipsy would dare to set foot on any part of Ellswood Park, but,' said Aunt Em solemnly, 'you never know.'

Chapter 9

In the first week of December Miss Nell and Kate drove into Chaxton to do their Christmas shopping. This was the first Christmas that Kate had money to spend on presents for the family, and she had enjoyed making a list of the things she intended to buy. Ladybird and the pony trap were left at the livery stables of the Rose and Crown and Miss Nell and Kate arranged to meet outside the Corn Exchange at four o'clock. The display of Christmas goods gave the shops a festive air and Kate's basket was soon filled with neatly wrapped parcels. There was a sewing box for Mary, dolls for Rose and May, a toy drum for Jimmy, and a box of lead soldiers for Teddy. She bought a box of lavender-scented soap for her mother and tobacco for Mr. Bassett. Her basket felt quite heavy as she made her way to the Corn Exchange. She arrived before Miss Nell and stood listening to three street musicians who were playing 'Good King Wenceslas'. They were wearing dark blue uniforms and peaked caps. Suddenly a man shouted 'That's a German band—how do we know that they're not spies?' and the people who had been listening to the music moved forward and formed a ring round the musicians and stared sullenly at them. The music ended abruptly and the three men looked uneasily at the crowd, and then a policeman came up and told the people to move on.

'You'd better be on your way too,' he said to the musicians, and they packed up their instruments and walked quickly away.

'They weren't doing any harm,' said a grey-haired man to Kate. 'I've got a son out in France, but I don't begrudge anyone making a bit of Christmas music. Some folk seem to be spy-crazy. There's an old clock-mender with a shop down by the close. All his windows were smashed by some hooligans last week—just because they saw the name Muller painted up over the shop door and they reckoned it was a German name. I don't know whether it is or not, but he's had that shop there ever since I can remember, and that's going back a main few years.'

Kate thought that the pleasure and excitement of the shopping expedition had been marred by the incident, but she did not say anything to Miss Nell as they drove home.

In the newspapers she was able to follow the course of the war. She read of the advances and retreats of the British Expeditionary Force, thinking of Sir Edward and the husband of Uncle Percy's sister Maude. Miss Nell went about her work looking anxious, and Kate was always relieved when she saw a letter from Sir Edward lying in the wire cage of the letter box. At school, instead of sewing lessons on Tuesday and Thursday afternoons, the girls were now busy knitting scarves and mittens in thick khaki wool which had been provided by Lady Margaret. In chapel on Sundays special prayers were said for the safety of the men away at the war. Sugar was beginning to be scarce in the shops, just as Aunt Em had predicted. Kate had tasted a cup of sugarless tea and was surprised to find that she really preferred it made that way.

One evening a carol-singing party arrived from the village. The vicar was there and also the verger with a lantern. Miss Nell had known that they would be coming and after they had sung they came into the hall for cups of cocoa and slices of cake. It was now almost nine months since Kate had left school and Mr. Willis did not recognize the tall girl in her black dress and white cap and apron who came behind Miss Nell with a heavy tray as Kate Bassett who had passed the Labour Examination.

Miss Nell had been giving Kate cookery lessons and on Christmas Eve she said that she could make the pastry for the mince pies. Kate thought that Miss Nell's pastry was always far lighter than hers, and Miss Nell could always make the pastry go farther than she could. At the first lesson both Miss Nell and Kate had used exactly the same amount of ingredients, but when the time came to cut the pastry into rounds for jam tarts, Kate could only make nine, while Miss Nell could make fourteen. The Christmas puddings had been mixed several weeks earlier and had been boiled in the copper in the scullery. They now stood on the top shelf of the dresser, topped with white cloths which Kate thought looked like butterfly wings. The Christmas cake was in the sideboard in the dining-room. As she carefully weighed the flour, Kate hoped that this would be one of her good pastry days.

When she awoke on Christmas morning she smiled ruefully when she saw that there was nothing at the foot of her bed. She was a working girl, now. She thought of the last Christmas when she had still been at school. In her stocking there had been an apple and an orange, and then a cornet-shaped packet of nuts, a pink sugar pig, a chocolate mouse, a clock-face made of icing sugar, liquorice bootlaces, chocolate drops, and small gifts of handkerchiefs and hair ribbons. She thought of the presents which she had received at previous Christmases. One year there was the wooden Dutch doll which was so like Aunt Em, and another time there was a wicker sewing basket with pins, needles, and cards of coloured thread. Once there had even been a blue and white doll's tea-set, but the Christmas which she always remembered most of all was when she was eight years old. On the morning of the Monday of the last week of school before they broke up for the holidays, Kate and Mary had been awakened by the sound of Aunt Em's voice saying that if they weren't careful they would be late for school. She had laughed at the surprise showing so clearly on their faces as they stared from the pillows to see her standing in the bedroom doorway.

'Your mother's not feeling very well this morning,' said Aunt Em, 'so be good girls and get dressed as quickly as you can.'

'How did you get here, Aunt Em?' asked Kate as she pushed back the bed-clothes.

'Never you mind,' said her aunt mysteriously, 'but just do as I tell you.'

Kate and Mary dressed quickly and then went downstairs to the kitchen where Aunt Em had bowls of porridge waiting for them. The porridge was rather lumpy and not at all like that which Mrs. Bassett made, but Aunt Em sat at the table and watched them eat it until the bowls were quite empty.

'Can we go upstairs before we go to school?' asked Kate.

'No, you can't,' said Aunt Em. 'What a child you are to be sure, Kate. There isn't time. Besides, I've got to do your hair.'

Kate wondered if Aunt Em had brought a new hair-brush from South Lodge. It felt as if it had been made of twigs and Aunt Em brushed the long braids of hair with heavy strokes.

'Keep still, child, do,' she said crossly, as Kate tried to twist her head from under her ungentle hands. Aunt Em strained the hair back far too tightly so that Kate almost cried with the pain. Mary was more fortunate when it was her turn because Aunt Em had just caught sight of the time from the clock on the mantelpiece and she gave Mary's hair only a small amount of brushing.

'There we are,' she said in a relieved voice as she tied the last bow. 'I've put your dinner in the basket, just like your mother does. Put your coats on and then hurry along to school or else you'll be late.'

She came out to the garden gate with the two girls and stared down the lane.

'I wish she would come on,' she said, speaking to no one in particular, and Kate and Mary walked slowly away, thinking that it was the most miserable Monday morning that they could ever remember. At the curve in the lane they met Mrs. Toogood with her lidded basket over her arm. She was a well-known figure in the village who often visited houses where there was any illness. She smiled and nodded at the two girls as she passed. Kate returned the smile only half-heartedly. There was always something mysterious about Mrs. Toogood and her old, black bonnet and gold ear-rings.

At dinner-time there was another disappointment for the two girls. Usually on Mondays there would be beef dripping from the roast joint of meat on Sunday, and Mrs. Bassett always made them tasty sandwiches for their dinner on the next day, but Aunt Em had either forgotten or did not know of this because she had simply packed a few slices of bread and butter.

'Is that all?' said Mary. 'No cake?'

'No,' said Kate sadly. 'Aunt Em must have forgotten.'

It was not a very happy time at school that day. Miss Crompton seemed even more cross than usual and caned one of the big boys who sat at the back of the classroom.

'And if there is any more noise,' she said, 'you will all stay in for an hour at four o'clock.'

The walk back to the cottage seemed very long. Before the Bassett girls had gone more than half-way, it began to rain and they both hoped that Aunt Em would have gone back to South Lodge and that when they reached home they would find Mrs. Bassett in the kitchen. Mary's lips quivered when Kate opened the back door and Aunt Em's voice told them to wipe their boots

on the sack which she had put by the doorstep. When they came into the kitchen she seemed to be in a very good humour.

'Well now,' she said, 'what do you think they've brought us?'

'A pony and trap?' said Mary, thinking of the long walk in the rain.

'A pony and trap?' repeated Aunt Em. 'Good souls alive, what would the likes of us want with a pony and trap? There's no room here for a trap, and who'd want a pony eating a body out of house and home?'

'Is it something to do with Mother?' asked Kate.

'Well, never mind about that now,' said Aunt Em, 'just go upstairs and see for yourself. Mind you knock on the bedroom door first.'

She came with them to the foot of the narrow, scrubbed staircase and watched as the two girls knocked on their mother's bedroom door.

'Come in,' called Mrs. Bassett, and they went inside. Aunt Em gave a small, satisfied smile and went back into the kitchen and began cutting bread and butter.

Kate and Mary stood just inside the bedroom door. For a moment they were too surprised to speak or move. Mrs. Bassett lay in bed nursing a newborn baby wrapped in a shawl and Mrs. Toogood sat in the chair by the fire with another baby in her arms.

'A new brother and sister,' said Mrs. Bassett.

'Your first Christmas presents,' said Mrs. Toogood, 'even if they are a week early.'

Kate smiled as she remembered how tiny the babies were. It seemed strange to think of them as being so small when they were now Jimmy and May and almost as tall as Rose who was two years older. She could still remember sitting on the bed in her mother's room until Aunt Em had called up the stairs to say that the tea was ready. It was the first and only time that she had ever seen a fire in any of the bedrooms, and when the lamp was lit the room seemed to be bathed in a golden glow which was reflected in the shining ear-rings of Mrs. Toogood, who, now that she was wearing a long, white apron and sitting in the chair by the fire, no longer seemed a strange and mysterious person, but instead appeared as the bright, cheerful-looking old lady that she really was.

When Kate and Mary went downstairs, Aunt Em was busy giving Teddy and Rose their tea.

'A brother and a sister—wasn't that a nice surprise?' she asked.

'Where did they come from?' said Mary.

'Ask me no questions and I'll tell you no lies,' said Aunt Em.

'Did Mrs. Toogood bring them?' said Kate. 'In that basket with the lid on?'

'Never mind about that now,' replied Aunt Em, taking a spoon out of two-year-old Rose's hand. 'Sit yourself down and be good children like Aunt Em says. I've cut a big plateful of bread and butter and there's a pot of my best plum jam.'

'Your plum jam tastes different,' said Mary, after a little while.

'Different from your mother's, you mean?' said Aunt Em with a smile. 'Well, I expect it does. I was always reckoned to be a good jam maker, though I do say it myself.'

The excitement of the last few days before Christmas was slightly dampened by the presence of Aunt Em, who was always telling the children to wipe their feet and not to make a noise. Even though Kate knew that her mother had already made the Christmas puddings and cake, it did not really seem like Christmas at all, and she wondered if the stockings would be filled that year.

Before she went to bed on Christmas Eve she had said to her father, 'Will this Christmas be the same as it always is?' and Mr. Bassett had looked up from the pair of boots he was mending and drew her towards him saying, 'The same as always, Kate,' and she had gone to bed with the same excitement that she always felt on Christmas Eve. Mr. Bassett was aware of Aunt Em's sharp ways, and grateful though he was for her help in the cottage, he looked forward to the time when Mrs. Bassett would be up and about again.

It was still dark when Kate awoke on Christmas morning, but she had felt at the bottom of the bed and there was a stocking and several small parcels. Then Mary woke up and they began whispering and soon afterwards Mr. Bassett came into the bedroom and lit the candle. For a while he stood watching as they explored the contents of the stockings and the parcels.

'The same as always, Kate?' he asked with a smile.

'Oh yes,' said Kate, holding up a pink sugar mouse. 'The best ever!'

Aunt Em did not approve of children waking up early in the morning, even if it was Christmas Day.

'I hope,' she said at breakfast-time, 'that you children realize how lucky you are. In my young days Father Christmas never brought me half as much as you found in those stockings of yours.'

At the end of Christmas week Mrs. Bassett came downstairs and Aunt Em returned to South Lodge.

'Those children need a really firm hand,' she said to Uncle Percy. 'Things were very different while I was there, I can tell you.'

Mr. Bassett and the children would have agreed with her. Aunt Em did not tell Uncle Percy how empty and quiet South Lodge had seemed when she unlocked the kitchen door and stood staring at the wilting potted plant on the window sill which he had forgotten to water while she was away.

Kate smiled as she thought once more of the first time that she had seen Jimmy and May. She glanced at the clock on the dressing-table. It was five minutes to six. She knew that her brothers and sisters would already be awake, exploring with eager hands the treasures that Father Christmas had brought. She thought of the Christmas tree standing in the parlour, decorated by Mrs. Bassett with the few remaining red and blue witch balls which were so fragile that each year another one was broken. There would be a tinsel star at the top of the tree and on the lower branches there would be spiral twists of silver paper and white-washed fir cones. On Christmas morning the children would discover that an unknown hand had added small packets of sweets.

On the day that school broke up there would have been a Christmas tree hung with presents given by Lady Margaret. The children would have formed a ring round the tree and sung all the well-known carols and then Lady Margaret would present each child with a gift which had been chosen and wrapped by Miss Crompton. At the end of the afternoon the vicar would call for three cheers for Lady Margaret who would smile in acknowledgement, and when the children had put on their hats and coats Miss Crompton and the vicar's wife stood at the door handing out a packet of sweets and an orange to each child. Last Christmas Miss Crompton had chosen *The Pilgrim's Progress* for Kate, one of the very few books she possessed and which had come with her to Penrose Farm.

When the Master and Miss Nell returned from the early celebration of Holy Communion, Miss Nell came into the kitchen with presents for Kate. From the Master there was a scarf which Kate had seen in one of the windows of Billington's, and Miss Nell gave her a pink and white dressing-table set similar to her own which Kate secretly admired each time she went into Miss Nell's room. Miss Grace and Mr. Hurford came to Christmas dinner and Miss Grace gave her a pair of gloves which matched the scarf the Master had given her.

'Leave the washing-up, Kate,' said Miss Nell, when she came out into the kitchen after dinner. 'Run upstairs and put on your hat and coat. Mr. Hurford will drive you home in the trap.'

The Bassetts were surprised when the trap drew up outside the garden gate and Kate stepped down from it.

'I'll call for you at about eight,' said Mr. Hurford, and from the window, Teddy watched enviously as he drove off with a flourish of his whip.

'Father Christmas has been,' said Rose, 'and he's brought lots of things.'

Kate admired everything he had brought. Her own gifts were very well received, especially the drum for Jimmy.

'There's something for you, too,' said Mary, and Mrs. Bassett gave Kate an old stocking which bulged excitingly. As she unwrapped the small parcels she was aware of her father and mother watching her. Even if she was the eldest daughter away in service, to them she was still only a child.

Aunt Em and Uncle Percy always came to Christmas tea and supper. This year, when Aunt Em opened the garden gate she was wearing a brown fur tippet which she had bought in Chaxton and then told Uncle Percy that it could be his Christmas present to her. Her gift to him was an ounce of tobacco. Aunt Em believed in giving only useful presents and so for the children there were gifts of stockings and underwear.

'Do you think there's any need to give Kate anything for Christmas, now that she's out at work and earning good money?' she had said to Uncle Percy.

'I don't see why not,' said Uncle Percy. 'Kate's a good girl.'

'Handsome is as handsome does,' Aunt Em had replied, and compromised by giving Kate an apron which she had bought for herself a long time ago, but which she had never used.

Uncle Percy was a man of few words and for most of the afternoon he sat quietly smoking by the fire. Aunt Em unbent sufficiently to play Snap and Happy Families with the children and was annoyed when she did not win a single game. She also wondered who had been foolish enough to buy the red and yellow drum which Jimmy banged so persistently. Her temper improved when Mrs. Bassett said that it was time for tea, and she watched closely as the best lace cloth was placed on the table and the best blue and white china was brought out.

Uncle Percy praised Mrs. Bassett's Christmas cake and seemed unaware of Aunt Em's grim expression. She admitted to herself that her sister-in-law's cake was very good, but thought that judging from the thickness of the slices she was cutting for everyone there would soon be none left. Aunt Em's own cake would be cut for Boxing Day tea. There would be a small slice for Uncle Percy and a small slice for herself. After that the cake would be put away in her yellow tin and only brought out when Uncle Percy asked for it, with the result that there was usually a large piece still in the yellow tin at Easter-time.

When everyone had finished tea and Mrs. Bassett and Kate began to clear the table, Aunt Em asked if there was anything she could do to help, but Mrs. Bassett said, 'No, you sit down, Em. Kate and I can manage, thank you,' which was exactly what she had hoped her sister-in-law would say. Kate and her mother were able to have a quiet talk in the kitchen over the washing-up without any interruptions from Aunt Em. Mr. Bassett told the children a story, sitting close to the lamp and making animal shadows on the wall with his hands, much to the annoyance of Aunt Em who wanted the lamp on her side of the table so that she could see to finish the grey worsted sock she was knitting for Uncle Percy. Even if it was Christmas Day, Aunt Em did not expect to sit with her hands folded in her lap.

Mrs. Bassett brought out fruit and nuts for everyone and elderberry wine for the grown-ups. When the story was ended, Mr. Bassett and Uncle Percy roasted chestnuts on the fire and Aunt Em moved the lamp so that the light shone on her steel knitting needles and grey wool, thankful that Jimmy had at long last stopped banging that drum and was now under the table with Teddy, playing with the lead soldiers. She glanced at Rose and May who were playing with their new dolls, and at her favourite, Mary, who was busily cracking hazel-nuts. She looked at Kate who sat back from the table just watching the others with an expression of quiet happiness on her face, and thought grimly that there must be a pile of work in Mrs. Bassett's mending basket large enough to keep both mother and daughter busy for a week. There must be plenty of knitting to do, too, if the children wore out their socks as quickly as their Uncle Percy did.

The twins had been allowed to stay up late because it was Christmas, but after May began to nod and Jimmy had been discovered asleep under the table with his face resting uncomfortably on the drum, Mrs. Bassett and Kate carried them upstairs. Jimmy did not wake up, and May was soon asleep when Kate tucked her up in her little bed which had been warmed by a hot brick wrapped in a piece of an old blanket. The rest of the evening passed very quickly and at five minutes to eight Kate put on her hat and coat and said good-bye to everyone. Waiting for Mr. Hurford at the gate, she felt rather forlorn as she looked back at the warm glow of the lamp in the parlour and at the faint light from the candle upstairs where Rose and Teddy were preparing for bed. It would be another two hours before Uncle Percy and Aunt Em set out for South Lodge.

'Have you had a good time, Kate?' asked Miss Grace, when she arrived with Mr. Hurford in the trap.

'Oh yes,' said Kate. 'I think that it's been the nicest Christmas ever.'

It was a clear, cold night and she was glad to have the old blanket Miss Grace had brought to tuck round her. The sky was full of stars, just as it must have been many years ago, she thought, when the shepherds were on the hills outside Bethlehem.

After the noise in the parlour at home, it seemed very quiet in the farm kitchen. Miss Nell had prepared a lavish supper of ham and chicken, with trifle to follow.

'Your mince pies were a great success, Kate,' she said. 'There are only two left.'

In her bedroom Kate arranged Miss Nell's Christmas gift on the dressing-table, placing the candlesticks on either side of the mirror and the hairpin holder and powder box on the tray with the ring tree in the middle. She wondered if there would ever be a time when she would have a ring to hang on one of its china branches.

Chapter 10

After Christmas the weather turned much colder.

'It's a main frost,' said the Master as he came along the passage for his breakfast. Because of the cold he was wearing an old sack round his shoulders and blowing on his fingers. Kate silently agreed. There had been a thin coating of ice on the water in the pink jug on her washstand. She was finding it hard to get up so early in the cold, dark mornings. She was always warm in bed because as well as the hot bricks which she put into the beds each evening, Miss Nell had given her two extra blankets from the chest on the landing. When Kate awoke in the mornings, she put out her hand and felt in the darkness for the box of matches, and when the candle had been lit she would look round the shadowed room and think how wonderful it would be if, just once in her life, she could sleep until nine o'clock and then open her eyes to see a brightly burning fire. She knew that it was a dream which was not likely to come true, because there was not even a fireplace in the attic. She would count up to a hundred and then with a determined effort push back the bed-clothes and another day would begin. She washed and dressed as quickly as she could. As she put up her hair, even her hairpins felt cold. Miss Nell had given her a piece of old blanket from the rag bag in the linen cupboard and with it she made a thick cross-over to put round her shoulders, but even then she shivered as she went downstairs to start work. She had chilblains on her fingers and they itched unbearably. They could not heal very quickly because she was unable to keep her hands really dry for very long periods. There was always so much scouring, washing-up, and scrubbing to be done. When she sat by the fire in the evenings the heat made the chilblains itch even more. Then Miss Nell gave her some pale green ointment which was wonderfully cool and soothing. Kate did not know its name, but she thought of it as the Balm of Gilead.

One morning during the last week in January, from the window of the dining-room she saw the postman coming up the garden path and she hurried into the hall and was just in time to see a letter falling into the wire cage of the letter box. For one moment she thought that it would be an extra letter from Sir Edward, but although it was addressed to Miss Nell, the letter did not bear a foreign stamp. Miss Nell was upstairs and when Kate took it to her she received it with such pleasure showing on her face that Kate wished that it had been from France. Later Miss Nell came into the dining-room where Kate was polishing and said that the letter was from Mr. Hurford. Miss Grace had badly scalded her hand.

'She wondered if you would like to go to Ringstone Farm for a week or two until she can use her hand again,' said Miss Nell. 'Would you like that, Kate?'

'Well, yes,' said Kate, 'but what about the work here?'

'I shall have to work a little harder while you're away,' said Miss Nell with a smile, 'but perhaps Mrs. Bray can come for two or three mornings. Finish the polishing,' she added, 'and then go upstairs and pack your clothes.'

It seemed strange to Kate to be folding dresses and counting stockings and handkerchiefs in the middle of the morning. She was just closing her trunk when Miss Nell called up the stairs to say that dinner was ready. Before he went back to work in the afternoon, the Master came into the kitchen.

'Off to fresh fields, Kate?' he said, and she felt in quite a holiday mood when Tom Collier brought Ladybird round to the side gate and lifted the trunk into the back of the trap.

'We'll go to your house first so that you can tell your mother what's happening,' said Miss Nell. 'I'm afraid that it will be too far for you to be able to go home on Sunday afternoons.'

Kate was able to spend a few minutes with her mother. Mrs. Bassett was surprised when she walked into the kitchen, but she was pleased that Miss Grace had asked for Kate to help her.

'It will be a change for you, Kate,' she said.

Aunt Em just happened to be looking out of the parlour window at South Lodge when the trap went by.

'I don't know whenever they get any work done at Penrose Farm,' she said to Uncle Percy. 'Young Kate seems to spend half her time careering round the countryside in that trap.'

She said the same thing to Mrs. Bassett on her next Sunday

afternoon visit and stared in surprise when her sister-in-law explained where Kate had gone.

'They must be pleased with Kate,' said Mrs. Bassett, with pardonable pride.

'Fancy,' replied Aunt Em, pursing her lips. 'Let's hope that she doesn't find that she's let herself in for more than she's bargained for.'

Miss Nell and Kate arrived at Ringstone Farm at half past three. The front door of the farmhouse was opened by Mrs. Hale, the wife of one of the farm men, and she led them into the sitting-room where Miss Grace was resting on the sofa.

'Thank you for coming so soon,' said Miss Grace. She looked rather pale and had her right hand in a sling. Kate went with Mrs. Hale into the kitchen and was shown where everything was kept.

'Mrs. Hurford said that she hoped that you'd be able to come over,' she said. 'I reckon that hand of hers must be real painful. I came up yesterday and this morning to get a bit of dinner ready, but it's a scrabble and no one can say any different. There's my husband and five children to see to. My eldest girl is nearly as tall as you are. When she leaves school at Easter, Mrs. Hurford says that there's a place for her here.'

It seemed rather strange to Kate to hear her refer to Miss Grace by her married name. Mrs. Hale helped her to carry her trunk upstairs. The attic rooms had still not yet been furnished, and so Kate was given one of the rooms on the first landing.

'It's a nice room,' said Mrs. Hale, and Kate agreed that it was, admiring the big, high brass bedstead with its white honeycomb pattern quilt and the mauve and white china on the washstand. There was a light-coloured dressing-table and wardrobe, and thick rugs on either side of the bed. The view from the window was different from the view at Penrose Farm. Instead of the open fields, the downs rose sharply behind the house, sheltering it from the January winds.

Mrs. Hale left soon afterwards and after Miss Nell had a cup of tea, she drove home at half past four. Miss Grace came into the kitchen and discussed the pattern of the work at Ringstone Farm.

'As I can use only one hand, I'm afraid that I'm not going to be able to do a great deal,' she said, 'but I'm sure that we'll be able to manage perfectly well together.'

The work was not very different from that at Penrose Farm.

During the next few days Kate rose at six, lit the fires, and carried brass cans of hot water upstairs. Mr. Hurford had an early morning cup of tea in the kitchen and then came back from the yard for breakfast in the dining-room with Miss Grace at eight o'clock. The doctor came to dress Miss Grace's hand. She had slipped on the wet floor of the dairy, and in trying to prevent herself from falling, she had overturned a bowl of boiling hot water.

Although she was quite confident of being able to do the house-work efficiently, Kate had been a little nervous of cooking the meals, but Miss Grace was always there to supervise, and except for a fruit cake which obstinately refused to rise, appetizing food was placed before Mr. Hurford when he came in at meal-times. Dinner at twelve o'clock was the main meal of the day, and after Mr. Hurford had gone back to work and the washing-up had been done, Kate was able to have a little time to herself. One afternoon she wrapped up warmly and followed the path up to the downs which led to the ring of stones. There were eight of them, each almost six feet in height. They seemed to Kate to have a forbidding, almost sinister air, and the wind blowing through the grass on the downs made her shiver. From where she stood she could look down at the farm and at the village where Miss Grace did her shopping, and after the grim outlines of the stones, the houses and barns seemed somehow reassuring.

One of the main differences at Ringstone Farm was that all the farm buildings were quite close to the house, and from the kitchen window Kate could look across the yard to the stables where there were two grey shire horses, Lightfoot and Blossom. At Penrose Farm, the yard was so far away that it was easy to forget that the house was part of a farm. Kate was glad that Mr. Hurford did not keep any geese to hiss and flap their wings at her when she went to collect the eggs.

One afternoon she went into the village to do some shopping for Miss Grace. It was about the same size as Bretherton, with side lanes leading off from the main street. Most of the houses were of grey stone with low, thatched roofs, but the blacksmith's forge was even older, with the black beams and dark red brick of Tudor times. The smith was busy at his anvil and she stopped for a moment to watch the sparks fly. From the narrow-windowed school close to the church came the sound of children singing, and Kate smiled when she recognized the song as one which Miss

Crompton had taught her pupils at Bretherton. The chapel was near the village pond and she saw from the notice board that a service was held every Sunday afternoon at three o'clock. The village shop was at the end of the main street, and when Kate went inside a grey-haired woman came to serve her.

'Are you in service up at Ringstone Farm?' she asked.

'Yes, I am,' said Kate with some surprise.

The woman smiled.

'I thought I recognized Mrs. Hurford's basket,' she said.

On her first Sunday Kate went to the afternoon service. Except for a big man with a beard who stood in the doorway handing out hymn-books, whom Kate recognized as the man she had seen working in the blacksmith's forge, it was almost like being at home in the chapel at Green Lane. There were the same yellow varnished pews and old harmonium, and the service was taken by Mr. Mitchell, the circuit minister.

'Hello, Kate,' he said afterwards. 'What brings you to this part of the world?'

When Kate told him that she was staying for a time at Ringstone Farm, Mr. Mitchell had a word with a pleasant-faced woman wearing a dark grey coat and hat, and she came over to speak to her.

'I'm Mrs. Hibberd,' she said pleasantly. 'The minister has been telling me about you. When I saw you come in, I wondered who you were. If you're going to be here next Sunday, perhaps you'll come and have tea with us. My daughter likes a bit of company. You'll be very welcome.'

'Thank you,' said Kate. She was grateful to Mrs. Hibberd for her kindness. The familiar hymn tunes had made her feel homesick as she thought of the same hymns being sung in the chapel in Green Lane.

Miss Grace readily agreed to let Kate go to Mrs. Hibberd's house to tea.

'I'm glad that you have been able to make a friend so soon,' she said.

On the following Sunday the bearded man was again handing out the hymn-books at the chapel.

'So you're the maid from Ringstone Farm,' he said. 'We'll see you after the service.'

Mrs. Hibberd was sitting in the front pew with her two grown-up sons and she turned and beckoned to Kate to go and sit with her. Kate walked up the aisle, conscious of the friendly, questioning glances of the other members of the congregation. The bearded man took the service.

'My husband,' whispered Mrs. Hibberd.

With his full, grey beard and deep, penetrating eyes, he was how Kate imagined that Moses must have looked. When the service ended, he stood at the door of the chapel and shook hands with each member of the congregation, just as Mr. Mitchell had done the previous week.

'Pleased to have you with us,' he said to Kate, as she came out into the January afternoon.

She waited with Mrs. Hibberd until the two sons, who were called Bill and Jack, had put the hymn-books away in a cupboard at the back of the chapel, and then Mr. Hibberd locked the front door. Mrs. Hibberd took her by the arm and they walked home. Kate hung back rather shyly when Mrs. Hibberd opened the front door of the blacksmith's house, and then she felt Mr.

Hibberd's large hand on her shoulder and he said, 'In you go, then, maid.'

'We're in the parlour because it's Sunday,' said his wife, and she led the way into a room where a young woman of eighteen lay on the sofa by a brightly burning fire.

'This is Kate I was telling you about, Liza,' said Mrs. Hibberd. 'Let me take your coat, lass, and then I'll see about the tea.'

'Come close to the fire and get warm, Kate,' said Liza.

Kate thought what a pretty girl Liza Hibberd was, with her big brown eyes and dark hair. She did not realize that her skin had that kind of transparency which comes from a lifetime of ill health. Bill and Jack disappeared and only Mr. Hibberd remained in the parlour with the two girls. As they talked quietly together, Kate soon forgot the large, bearded figure sitting in the armchair as she began to answer Liza's questions. Liza was interested in everything that Kate had to say about her brothers and sisters, and her work at Penrose Farm. She herself thought that her life was rather ordinary. She knew it was no different from that of other girls of her age, but to Liza it seemed as fresh and new as a story from the books which Mrs. Treharne, the doctor's wife, lent her. When Kate said that she had been up on the downs to see the ring of stones, Liza told her that in one of Mrs. Treharne's books they were called the eight dancing maidens.

'There's a legend that a long time before even the Romans came to Britain, eight girls went up to the downs to offer garlands of flowers to the gods of the hills. The gods of the trees were angry because the girls hadn't brought any flowers for them, and so in revenge, as the girls danced, they turned them into stones. It's only a story of course,' Liza said with a smile, seeing the serious expression on her visitor's face, but Kate remembered the strange feeling that she had when she stared at the ring of stones, and how comforting the farm and the village had seemed.

Liza took a sewing bag from the back of the sofa and showed Kate her embroidery.

'How beautiful,' said Kate. 'I'm not very good at sewing, and then it's only ordinary hemming that I do. I could never master anything like that.'

'It helps to pass the time,' said Liza quietly. The blacksmith watched the two girls sitting in the twilight, his own daughter so delicate and pale on the sofa, and the bright, sturdy girl by her side.

106

He was proud of the strength of his sons, but Liza held a special place in his heart.

Mrs. Hibberd appeared with the lamp and began to lay the table for tea, and then Bill and Jack came in and the small parlour seemed to be uncomfortably full as they were as tall and broad-shouldered as their father. Kate was glad when Mrs. Hibberd said that she and Liza would have their tea at a small table by the fire. She stayed with the Hibberds until it was seven o'clock, and then regretfully rose to leave.

'I think you've done our Liza good,' said Mrs. Hibberd, when Kate was putting on her coat. 'Perhaps you'll come again next Sunday afternoon, if you're able.'

'Yes, I will, thank you,' said Kate. 'I'd like to.'

Mrs. Hibberd looked at her intently and smiled.

Mr. Hibberd had said that Bill and Jack would walk back to Ringstone Farm with Kate, and when she had said good-bye to Liza they were waiting for her in the passage with a lantern. They both had the same stern manner as their father and they walked on either side of her, making her feel that she was almost a prisoner. They made no attempt at conversation, and Kate herself could not think of anything to say. She was aware of a feeling of relief as she wished them good night at the back door of the farm.

'Thank you for walking me home,' she said.

'You're welcome,' said Jack gruffly, and then the two men moved away in the darkness. Kate stood looking after them until the glow of the lantern faded into the distance, and as she went into the kitchen she thought how sad it must be for Liza to have to lie on the sofa all day in the parlour. It was so easy to take for granted the gift of health and strength.

The next afternoon she was busy ironing when someone tapped at the kitchen door and she opened it to find a pedlar with a basket of haberdashery standing there.

'Anything the ladies need?' he said in a wheedling voice. He was an old man with a black patch over his right eye. The basket was filled with all sorts of things. Kate looked at the cards of lace and thought how coarse they seemed when compared with her own crocheted edgings, but she bought a pair of bootlaces and Miss Grace bought a comb and a packet of hairpins.

'Is there anything the menfolk want?' said the pedlar. 'Laces, knives, collar studs, watch chains?'

'At this time of day all the men are at work in the yard,' said Miss Grace.

'Thank you, lady,' said the pedlar, and he went away smoking an old clay pipe.

In the evening after supper Kate had toothache. The tooth was not loose, and so Miss Grace found an old linen bag and Kate filled it with salt and then heated it in the oven, just as Mrs. Bassett always did at home. With the warm bag held against her cheek she found a certain relief from the pain. Before she went to bed she heated the bag of salt again and went to sleep with it against her face, but she awoke later with the pain as violent as before. She lit her candle and saw from the clock on the dressing-table that it was just one o'clock. She drew back the curtains and looked out. It was a clear night and the downs seemed to rise silvery grey in the moonlight. For the first time she realized that in the half light the ring of stones really did resemble human figures, and she thought again of the legend of the eight dancing maidens. Her cheek throbbed unbearably and she decided to go downstairs and reheat the bag of salt. As at Penrose Farm, the fire in the range was kept in all night. Pulling on her coat over her night-gown and reaching for her slippers, she came out on to the landing and went downstairs to the kitchen, glad when she saw the dull, red glow of the fire behind the bars of the range. The oven was quite warm as she placed the bag on the top shelf and put some more coal on the fire. As she sat down to wait for it to burn up, the silence of the night was broken only by the ticking of the clock on the mantelpiece and the neighing of the horses in the stable. She went to the window and looked out. She was surprised when she saw that a mist was forming in the yard, because a few minutes earlier when she had looked out of her bedroom window she had been able to see the ring of stones quite clearly. Again there was the neighing of the horses, and then she realized that it was not mist in the yard at all. It was smoke. She unbolted the back door and ran across the yard to the stable, wrenching the door open. Part of the door was already in flames, and a pile of hay inside was burning fiercely. The stable was full of smoke. She snatched up a pitchfork and began to clear a pathway through the burning hay to where the two horses were stamping in their stalls and straining at their halters. As she approached Lightfoot, he kicked backwards with a great flash of iron-clad hooves.

'It's all right,' Kate shouted through the smoke. 'It's all right,' and she struggled to untie the halter. The horse stood quietly for a moment and Kate began to lead him towards the door, but the sight of the flames terrified him and he suddenly reared up on his hind legs with such force that Kate was almost dragged into the the air. She felt a searing pain as the leather strap was pulled from her hand, and she overbalanced and fell on the floor in front of the horse. In a daze she looked up to see Lightfoot towering above her, his great, staring eyes and flashing teeth making him seem like a creature from a nightmare. There was the glint of iron as his hooves came down towards her. With a little sob she rolled towards one side, putting her hands to her face. Then she heard the crash of the horse's hooves on the stable floor. For a while she lay in the hay, afraid to move. When at last she dared to look at the horse, he was backing towards the second stall where Blossom was still tied by his halter.

'Come on, Lightfoot, please!' shouted Kate despairingly, and then she took off her coat and placed it over his head. She caught hold of the halter strap again, pulling with all her strength, and suddenly the horse began to walk towards the door, no longer afraid now that he could not see the flames. Together they walked past the burning hay and came out into the cold night air. Mr. Hurford had been awakened by the sound of the horses and the banging of the kitchen door which Kate had left unfastened, and he ran across the yard just as Kate was coming from the stable with Lightfoot.

'Take the coat,' she said, and he snatched it from Lightfoot's head and ran into the stable. Kate heard him calling to Blossom and there was an answering whinny from inside his stall. She stood in the yard with Lightfoot. Somehow she had lost her slippers, but in spite of the cold she did not realize that her feet were bare and that she was wearing only a night-gown. She was only aware of a great warm feeling of relief as Mr. Hurford led Blossom out through the stable door. She took the horse's halter from him and stood watching as the farmer ran backwards and forwards moving the burning hay from the stable out into the yard. Then he ran to the duckpond and staggered across the yard with a bucket of water in each hand. As Kate stood between the horses she lost count of the number of times that he filled the buckets from the pond, but it seemed a long time before he said, 'I think it'll be all right now, Kate.'

Then Miss Grace came out into the yard and at the sound of her voice Kate turned to face her. Everything seemed to spin and she felt herself falling.

Afterwards Mr. Hurford told Miss Grace that he would always remember the sight that met his eyes as he came into the yard. Kate seemed a ghost-like figure in her long, white night-gown, and with Lightfoot's face covered by her coat, it looked as if she was leading a headless horse. Kate did not know that, of course. She vaguely remembered having been carried upstairs and having something hot to drink and that was all. When she awoke in the morning she was horrified to see that it was ten past nine. She began to push back the bed-clothes and then Miss Grace said, 'Breakfast in bed today, Kate,' and Mrs. Hale came in with a tray.

'Are you all right, Kate?' asked Miss Grace anxiously.

'Why, yes,' said Kate. 'And my toothache's gone.'

Mr. Hurford was not sure how the fire could have started. None of his men smoked, but he had a suspicion that the pedlar had hung around the stable with his old clay pipe.

'I don't expect that we shall see him around this way again,' he said grimly, when he came in for dinner.

The two horses seemed none the worse for their fright, and when Kate went into the yard in the afternoon, two men were putting a new door on the stable.

'I reckon you saved the lives of the horses,' said one of the men. 'You must be a quick-witted maid.'

'It was the toothache, really,' said Kate, feeling rather shy.

'I'd say that it was more than that,' said the man.

The news of the fire at Ringstone Farm soon reached the village.

'Been having some adventures up at the farm, then, from what I hear,' said Mr. Hibberd as he gave Kate her hymn-book when she went to chapel on Sunday. As she walked up the aisle to where Mrs. Hibberd was sitting, she was aware of whispering and admiring glances from the congregation. Mrs. Hibberd smiled and pressed her hand, and even Bill and Jack looked at her and grinned.

'You're a real live heroine,' said Liza, when Kate went into the parlour at the blacksmith's house.

'At the time I felt anything but brave,' said Kate.

'All the same,' said Mr. Hibberd. 'I reckon you must have been.

We know the strength of those shire horses, don't we, lads?' and Bill and Jack nodded in solemn agreement.

One evening Mr. Hurford's parents came to supper at Ringstone Farm, and Miss Grace was anxious that the meal should be a success. Kate thought how splendid the dining-room table looked with the white table napkins in mother-of-pearl rings and the green and gold dinner service which had been part of the wedding present from Miss Nell. It was the first time that she had waited at table, and she was rather nervous at the beginning of the meal, but Miss Grace gave her little nods of encouragement, and she soon found that she was able to walk round the table carrying the plates and vegetable dishes as calmly as if she had been doing it all her life. After supper Mrs. Hurford came out into the kitchen where Kate was washing up and praised the damson pie.

'You've a fine light hand with pastry,' she said, 'and a light sleeper too,' she added with a twinkle in her eye. 'I've just been hearing about the fire.'

Miss Grace was now able to use her right hand again and it was arranged that Kate should return to Penrose Farm on Saturday. On the Friday she went to say good-bye to Liza Hibberd.

'Perhaps you'll write to me if you have the time,' said Liza.

'Yes,' replied Kate. 'I'd like to.'

'And if ever you're this way again,' said Mrs. Hibberd, 'please feel free to come and see us.'

Bill and Jack were not there that evening and so Mr. Hibberd walked back to the farm with Kate. At the kitchen door he took her hand in his and said quietly, 'God bless you, lass,' and then he strode away into the night.

On Saturday afternoon Mr. Hurford and Miss Grace drove back to Penrose Farm with Kate and her trunk in the back of the trap. In her purse there were two sovereigns from Mr. Hurford, and Miss Grace arranged with Miss Nell that there would also be a new winter coat for her to be made by Mrs. Hives.

Chapter 11

Kate was glad to be back with Miss Nell. She had enjoyed her stay with Miss Grace, but she was beginning to think with affection of Penrose Farm, not with the same depth of feeling as she would always think of her parents' cottage, but it was with a sense of homecoming that she went about her work. Although she was not quite sure how she would explain away the apparent extravagance of the new winter coat which was being made by Mrs. Hives, she had not intended to say anything about the fire at Ringstone Farm to her parents, but her mother and father already knew what had happened. Mr. Bassett had gone with Mr. Blake, his employer, to a cattle market which had also been attended by Mr. Hurford and he had gone over to the sheep-pen where Mr. Bassett was inspecting some ewes and told him of Kate's bravery.

'She really is a quick-thinking girl,' he said.

Aunt Em found out about it, of course, and said to Mrs. Bassett that Kate had no business to be wandering about the house in the middle of the night.

'She might have caught her death of cold,' she said. 'Then she'd have been sorry. I don't know what the next generation is coming to.'

The postman still brought letters for Miss Nell, and Kate was proud to be the only person to know that they were from Sir Edward. Remembering her promise to Liza Hibberd, she began to write to her. Liza was always interested in news of life at the farm. Spending all day on the sofa in the parlour, she had read a great many books which the doctor's wife lent her, but she told her mother that Kate's letters were far more entertaining than some of the volumes from Mrs. Treharne's bookcase. In one letter Kate told her about the lambing season, and how pleased the Master was that not one of the new-born lambs was lost, in spite of the cold winds. She began to keep a diary, writing down the day's events on odd scraps of paper until she bought a notebook in Chaxton. In March the great event in the farmhouse was the spring-cleaning, and she told Liza how Mrs. Bray came to the farm every morning for two weeks to help with all the extra work. The carpets were taken up and hung over the clothes-lines in the back garden and Kate and Miss Nell, wearing old aprons and holland mob-caps to protect their hair from the dust, beat them with large fan-shaped beaters. Floors were scrubbed and the boards polished with a special lavender-scented wax which Miss Nell made from a recipe which had been handed down from her great-grandmother. All the mirrors were washed with a damp sponge and then dusted with finely sifted whitening powder and then polished with an old silk handkerchief. The china and glass-ware were washed by Kate, and Mrs. Maslen came to wash the curtains and the extra blankets. The shelves in all the cupboards and wardrobes were relined with fresh paper and Tom Collier came one afternoon and whitewashed the ceiling and walls of the dairy. Kate wrote to Liza saying that everything had to be made clean and spotless for the spring, and Mrs. Hibberd smiled under-standingly when Liza read that part of the letter to her. The same activity was going on in all the houses in Bretherton. At Ellswood Park, while Lady Margaret went to London for two weeks with Miss Louise, the maids swept, scoured, and polished under the accusing eye of the housekeeper. Mrs. Bassett was equally busy in the cottage. The only person in the village quite unmoved by the fever of spring-cleaning was Aunt Em at South Lodge.

'I don't believe in spring-cleaning,' she said scornfully, looking grimly at the lines of extra washing blowing in the March breezes in the back gardens. 'If people did their work thoroughly and properly each week, there would be no need for such carryings-on.'

In one of her letters Liza told Kate that her brothers, Bill and Jack, had enlisted in the Army and were together with a cavalry regiment at Aldershot. Mrs. Hibberd had tried hard to persuade them not to go, but after a long talk with her husband she had said no more and tried to keep her voice firm and steady as she wished them good-bye when they set out for the enlisting office at Chaxton. Mr. Hibberd then employed a young lad, Victor Smith, as an apprentice. He was an orphan boy from the work-house, and Liza wrote saying that she thought that Mrs. Hibberd found a certain happiness in treating Victor as if he were a third son. This was quite true. She had liked the shy, pale-faced boy the first time that she had seen him standing uncertainly in the forge, warming his hands at the blacksmith's fire. When he went up to bed after eating the largest supper he could ever remember, there was a hot brick wrapped in a piece of old flannel in his bed. Victor had never known such luxury. Mr. Hibberd was pleased with the eager way in which he went to work.

'He's got a way with the horses,' he said to Mrs. Hibberd after his first week's work at the forge.

'Yes, he's a good lad,' said his wife. Her secret ambition was to make him as big and strong as her own two soldier sons.

At Chaxton two of the clergy houses in the close were being used as a military hospital, and when Kate and Miss Nell drove in to do the weekly shopping they often saw soldiers in the streets.

'They look so young,' said Miss Nell.

Once Kate saw two soldiers walking slowly together. One had a white walking-stick and the right sleeve of the tunic of his companion was empty and pinned to the flap of his pocket. She felt very sad when she realized that they had gone to the war as young, strong men and had come back to England so terribly changed. She wondered where they would go and what would happen to them when the time came for them to leave the hospital.

She came downstairs at six o'clock to a fine morning in April, smiling as she glanced at the zinc baths in which the fortnightly wash had been soaking overnight in readiness for Mrs. Maslen. She knew what the washerwoman would say when she arrived. 'Well, it looks as if it will be a fine drying day.'

Unless it was actually raining, it was what she said each time that she came to the farm. The Master and Miss Nell were still at breakfast in the dining-room when she came into the kitchen.

'Good morning, Mrs. Maslen,' said Kate.

'Morning, maid,' said Mrs. Maslen. She sat down and stared for a moment at the pair of her husband's boots she always wore. Then she said, 'Have you heard the news from Ellswood Park?'

'No,' said Kate.

'It's Sir Edward,' said Mrs. Maslen. 'He's been killed in France.'

It seemed to Kate that the brightness of the day was suddenly dimmed, almost as if someone had turned down a lamp and left a room in semi-darkness. She thought of Miss Nell in the dining-room and she knew that she must tell her what had happened before Mrs. Maslen did. She glanced at the clock. The Master would soon have finished his breakfast and would be going back to the farmyard, so she moved towards the kitchen door, waiting to hear the sounds of his footsteps in the passage.

'Lady Margaret is in a bad way over it, as you can imagine,' said Mrs. Maslen. 'They've sent up to London for Miss Louise.'

Kate heard the dining-room door being opened and she waited to hear the Master go by. Then she realized that it was Miss Nell's quick, light step coming along the passage and she hurriedly opened the kitchen door, hoping that she would be in time to prevent her from coming into the room, but she was too late. Miss Nell stood in the doorway with the breakfast tray.

'Good morning, Miss Nell,' said Mrs. Maslen. 'I've just been telling young Kate here. They've just heard up at Ellswood Park that Sir Edward's been killed.'

'I'll take the tray, Miss Nell,' said Kate, moving so that Mrs. Maslen could not see Miss Nell's face. She stared at Kate, her face very white, and the cups on the tray rattled in their saucers until Kate reached out and took the tray from her shaking hands.

'When did it happen?' said Miss Nell, coming to the table.

'I don't know for sure,' said Mrs. Maslen. 'I only heard about it last night. Mrs. Davis lives next door to me. Her daughter Annie works in the kitchen at the Park, and she came down last night to tell her, and then Mrs. Davis banged on the kitchen wall for me to go in and hear all about it. It's a shame and no mistake. He was such a well-set-up chap, too, not so grand in his manner as Lady Margaret, but what I'd call a real gentleman.'

Kate watched Miss Nell as Mrs. Maslen, unaware of the pain she was causing her, went on talking.

'I remember once,' she said 'that I was coming along from old Mr. Kensett's cottage, and Sir Edward overtook me and gave me a lift in the trap. He took me right home—all the way through the village—and there was I sat up next to him like a lady, not knowing where to look as folk were curtsying as we went by.'

She sighed.

'And now he's gone for ever. I don't know what the world is coming to, what with the war and everything. I tell you, it took all the heart out of me when I heard about it. And I shouldn't be surprised if there isn't some fine young lady somewhere who'll be crying her eyes out when she hears the news.'

There was silence in the kitchen for a few minutes. Mrs. Maslen sighed again.

'Well, this won't do,' she said heavily. 'I must make a start, I suppose.'

She went into the scullery and shut the door. Miss Nell sat at the kitchen table so still that Kate was afraid. She filled a glass with water and set it before her.

'Thank you, Kate,' said Miss Nell in such a gentle voice that Kate began to cry. She cried for Sir Edward, dead in France, for Lady Margaret in her great house at Ellswood Park, but most of all she cried for Miss Nell sitting at the kitchen table, so white and ill.

'It's all right, Kate,' said Miss Nell, putting her hand on her shoulder, but her voice trembled. Kate reached up for her hand.

'Oh, Miss Nell, I'm so sorry,' she said.

'I know, my dear,' replied Miss Nell.

Sadly Kate went into the dairy and started working, and Miss Nell began to wash up the breakfast things. Mrs. Maslen came in from the scullery.

'Was that young Kate crying like that about Sir Edward?' she said. 'What a tender-hearted girl she must be.'

'Yes, she is,' said Miss Nell.

'And a young demon for work, too,' went on Mrs. Maslen. 'Did you see the way she jumped up for the tray the minute you came in?'

As Kate washed the red tiles of the dairy floor, she thought of the afternoon when she and Miss Nell had gone to pick dandelions and Sir Edward had been standing in the lane. She remembered how he had helped her over the stile, while Miss Nell stood by holding the baskets. She thought of Miss Grace, Mrs. Hurford now, and living happily at Ringstone Farm. Perhaps Miss Nell might one day have been Lady Ellen, going to the school by the church to call the register every Wednesday morning. And now Sir Edward was dead and any plans which he and Miss Nell had made for the future were at an end.

Wearily she went back into the kitchen. Miss Nell was not there. She went quietly up the stairs. The room of Miss Nell's door was shut, but Kate could hear the sound of her weeping. She longed to open the door and go in, but she knew that Miss Nell must be alone with her grief, so she went back downstairs and continued with her work, hurrying so that she could go on with Miss Nell's.

She made a cottage pie and a rice pudding. Miss Nell came into the kitchen just after eleven o'clock and saw the preparations she had made.

'Thank you, Kate,' she said. 'You're a good girl.'

The Master had already heard the news from his men. When he came home at twelve o'clock Kate thought how hard it must be for Miss Nell to have to sit in the dining-room listening to what her father had to say and trying all the time to behave as if Sir Edward had been known to her only by name. After her morning's work, Mrs. Maslen was ready to continue talking about the family at Ellswood Park when she came into the kitchen for her dinner.

'You wouldn't remember Sir Charles, would you, Kate?' she said. 'That would be Sir Edward's father. He was killed in a hunting accident. Well, rich or poor, we all get our troubles in this world. There's been Careys at Ellswood Park for hundreds of years.'

Kate thought that she had never known such a long day. The work seemed dreary and hard and she was glad when it was time to go to bed. She thought too, how Miss Nell must long for the night to come so that she could be alone.

Because she knew that she would always remember the kindness that Miss Nell had shown her during the first weeks at the farm when everything seemed so strange, Kate tried hard to think of ways in which she could show her sympathy for Miss Nell in her grief. On Sunday evening as she walked back to the farm after her half day, she picked a few primroses and arranged them in a blue and white egg cup and placed it on the mantelpiece in the kitchen. Miss Nell saw the flowers, and looked at Kate and nodded her thanks.

At the end of the month a memorial service was held for Sir Edward at the parish church. The Master went, wearing the same dark suit that he had worn at Miss Grace's wedding. Miss Nell and Kate spent the evening sewing in the kitchen. They both made attempts at conversation, but there were often long pauses when their thoughts were far away, and there was the gleam of tears in Miss Nell's eyes. During the days that had followed that terrible morning, Kate greatly admired the courage that Miss Nell showed. She was certain that the Master did not realize that Sir Edward was the man whom his daughter had loved. When he was there she seemed as bright and cheerful as she always had been, but when

Kate took up the hot water each morning, she was always awake, as if she had been unable to sleep for thinking of Sir Edward, who would never come back.

When Kate went home on Sunday afternoon, Aunt Em was already sitting in the parlour, telling Mrs. Bassett about the memorial service. Her sharp eyes had missed nothing.

'The church was packed right out, every pew full to bursting,' she said. 'Everyone was wearing mourning of some sort, even if it was only a black armband. And that Lady Margaret, you should have seen her. She held herself so stiff and straight. She was like a queen in her black dress and long veil. Not like that Miss Louise. Once or twice I thought that she was going to faint.'

'I wonder what Lady Margaret will do now?' said Mrs. Bassett.

'I suppose she was only staying at the Park until Sir Edward married,' said Aunt Em, 'and then she'd have moved into the Dower House. I dare say that quite a few had been setting their cap at him in their time, even if I don't care to name any names.'

She glanced at Kate who was sitting with May on her lap.

'I saw that Farmer Linden was there, which was no more than it should have been, seeing that he's a tenant and all. He sat quite near the front of the church, too. As I said to your Uncle Percy, you'd have thought that the Park people would have had pride of place at a time like that. After all, working for the gentry, we count for more than just tenants. Still, there it is. Mind you,' Aunt Em went on, turning again to Mrs. Bassett, 'I think that old Aaron Leeves is getting a bit past the verger's job. Some of the brass in the church looked as if it could have done with a good polishing. I expect that the only reason that the vicar lets him stay on is because his daughter Maggie works in the vicarage kitchen. Do you know, if I hadn't been a bit sharp and stepped forward, he would have let that Mrs. Croucher sit in front of me, and she only the wife of the fourth keeper up at the North Lodge where no one ever goes from one month's end to another. She was wearing a hat that I wouldn't have put on a scarecrow. I tell you, if you don't spur up for yourself nowadays, you'll soon find yourself in the workhouse.'

Kate realized that in spite of grief, people somehow were able to go on with the tasks of everyday life. At Penrose Farm Miss Nell worked in the farmhouse and continued to teach Kate her household skills. Mary said that Lady Margaret still came to the school each Wednesday at eleven o'clock. She was an even more frightening figure now that she wore a black dress and a mourning veil.

She gave a stained-glass window as a memorial to Sir Edward, and the day after it had been dedicated, Kate went into the church to see it. Mr. Leeves was dusting the pews at the front of the nave, and he looked up as she pushed open the heavy oak door.

'Come to see the window, then, maid?' he said. 'It's a right beautiful thing, isn't it? It came all the way from London, every single piece of it. Did you ever see such colouring?'

It really was a beautiful window. As Kate stood gazing in admiration, the sun came from behind a cloud and the colours seemed to glow with life. She suddenly realized that the window faced in the direction of Penrose Farm, and she wondered if Miss Nell would realize this and gain any comfort from it when she went to Holy Communion every Sunday.

'Well, look at that,' said Mr. Leeves. 'How did that get there?' He pointed to the long stone sill of the window which bore a brass plate with Sir Edward's name on it. Someone had placed a spray of blackthorn blossom on the window ledge.

'I must have that off before Lady Margaret sees it, or else there'll be the devil to pay.'

Kate remembered that in the afternoon Miss Nell had driven down into the village.

'Can't you leave it?' she said. 'It looks so pretty.'

'I suppose so,' said the verger. 'All the same, I'd like to know who put it there.'

Chapter 12

'Have you heard the news?' asked Aunt Em, when she arrived at the cottage one Sunday afternoon.

Without waiting for either her brother or Mrs. Bassett to reply, she went on, 'Still, I don't suppose that you have. I only heard last night, myself. Living up here right out of the village, you're bound to be rather out of things. I've always said that. I can't think why you don't move down into the village when a house becomes empty.'

'What news?' said Mrs. Bassett patiently.

'Lady Margaret,' said Aunt Em, 'is selling up. She's selling Ellswood Park and all the estate with it—even the Dower House.'

'Where does she intend to live then?' Mrs. Bassett asked.

'Well, they do say that she's going up to London to live with Miss Louise,' replied Aunt Em, 'but how anyone would want to go and live in a place like that beats me. It took my breath away when Percy came home and told me. I couldn't believe it at first. But it's true right enough. We've all had instructions that there's a Mr. Eliot coming to look over everything next week, and he'll want to inspect the lodge houses and see all the farms and cottages on the estate.'

'It sounds as if he means business,' said Mr. Bassett.

'I suppose so,' said Aunt Em, 'unless he turns out to be a Paul Pry, and just wants to come poking his nose into everything without having any real intention of buying. There's plenty of that kind about. Still, he'll be welcome to step inside South Lodge any time without giving notice. As I said to Percy, there's nothing there that won't bear the light of common day—which is more than you can say for some people. I dare say that quite a few will be running round with a dustpan and brush, unless I'm very much mistaken. Still, I shall be ready any time this Mr. Eliot likes to call.'

Mr. Mason, the Ellswood Park estate agent, had already been to Penrose Farm to tell Mr. Linden of the impending visit.

'There's not much I can tell you at the moment,' he said to the Master and Miss Nell, as they sat in the drawing-room with glasses of dandelion wine, 'but from what I hear this Mr. Eliot is looking for a country house. He's not really very interested in the outlying farms, so there'll be no cause for you to go worrying unnecessarily.'

'Do you think that the sale will go through?' said the Master.

'I think it will,' said Mr. Mason, 'but whatever he decides, Mr. Eliot will make up his mind fairly quickly.'

'The sooner the better,' said the Master.

Aunt Em secretly looked forward to Mr. Eliot's visit. Although she would never have admitted it to anyone, she was often very lonely at South Lodge. Uncle Percy's work kept him out in the parklands and coverts for long periods, and when her work was done, Aunt Em was quite pleased to have to come out and open the gates for Lady Margaret's carriage, although she pretended that it was a great nuisance to be interrupted just when she was busy in the middle of doing something. On Monday morning she got up an hour earlier than usual, and was able to have most of the washing done before Uncle Percy came downstairs for his breakfast.

'You're an early bird,' he said.

'Handsome is as handsome does,' said Aunt Em blandly.

When all the washing was hung out to dry, Aunt Em made a fruit cake, using her Christmas recipe. She had considered carefully whether she would be justified in using some of the dried fruit from her secret store cupboard, but finally decided that a fruit cake was very often better for keeping, just like wine, and that it would not be an unnecessary extravagance. She washed her best tea service and polished the oak tray with brass handles which had been given to Uncle Percy by his grandmother. In the afternoon she changed into her Sunday dress and sat in the kitchen, waiting with a sense of pleasurable anticipation. Several times she went to the window and looked out, but no one came, and her feeling of pleasure changed to one of disappointment. At half past four she realized that Mr. Eliot would not be calling at South Lodge that day, and she went angrily upstairs to change back into her blouse and skirt, thinking of the pile of ironing she could have done that afternoon, but would now have to do that evening. Uncle Percy was surprised, when after the tea had been cleared away, she put the flat-irons on the range to heat, and with a great sigh took her ironing blanket from the cupboard.

'Your early start didn't seem to do you much good,' he said.

'Well, never mind about that,' said Aunt Em, 'but even if grand folks may be thinking of buying the estate, there are some people who have work to do. I dare say that you'd be the first to complain if you went to your drawer and there wasn't a clean shirt to be found.'

Uncle Percy recognized the danger signals in the tone of Aunt Em's voice and went out into the scullery to split some firewood.

On Tuesday afternoon Aunt Em again changed into her Sunday dress and sat in the kitchen waiting for the visitors. No one came.

'Has anyone been?' said Uncle Percy, when he came home for his tea.

'No,' said Aunt Em crossly, 'and no one can be expected to sit around all day for ever, waiting until they're good and ready to call. Whether they've been or not, I'm going into Chaxton on Thursday, and if he calls while I'm out, this high and mighty Mr. Eliot can either like it or lump it.'

On the third afternoon Mr. Mason arrived with two men. As she opened the front door of South Lodge in answer to Mr. Mason's knock, Aunt Em stared at the two men who accompanied him. One was big and squarely built, wearing a grey suit and highly polished boots and leggings. He wore a rose in his button-hole, and his walking-stick was tipped with what Aunt Em was almost certain was gold. Not what I would call real gentry, she thought, as she curtsied stiffly, real gentry don't make such a show with their money. She was not in the least impressed by the third man. He was tall and thin, wearing a brown suit and carrying a red notebook in his hand.

'Good afternoon, Mrs. Potter,' said Mr. Mason. 'I've brought Mr. Eliot and Mr. Reynolds from London to see over the house.'

'Good afternoon,' said Aunt Em, indicating a sack by the door where boots, highly polished or not, could be wiped. When she was quite satisfied that the three pairs of boots were clean, she led the three men down the passage into the kitchen, hoping that they would be suitably impressed by the shining black-leaded range, the scrubbed kitchen table, and the blue and white china on the dresser.

'This is a pleasant room,' said Mr. Eliot.

He talks like a foreigner, thought Aunt Em. She agreed calmly that it was, as he had said, a pleasant room, and watched with narrowed eyes as the third man, Mr. Reynolds, wrote something in his red notebook.

'And now the front room, perhaps,' said Mr. Mason.

'You mean the parlour,' replied Aunt Em, taking her purse from the kitchen mantelpiece and searching for the key. She unlocked the door, and stood on the threshold facing her visitors. No one ever entered the parlour except Aunt Em, and the three men could only glance over her broad shoulders and see the mantelpiece draped with a short red plush curtain with a bobble fringe and a row of china ornaments.

'Beautifully kept,' murmured the agent, with a glance at Mr. Eliot.

'Thank you,' said Aunt Em, allowing herself a small smile as she relocked the door.

'And if we could go upstairs,' said Mr. Mason.

Aunt Em obligingly led the way, confident that the brass knobs on the bedsteads would be the brightest that they had seen for many a day, and that the patchwork quilt in the back bedroom would put Joseph's coat of many colours to shame. She was rather annoyed that Mr. Eliot passed no comment on the furniture, but merely admired the view from the windows, and she again noticed that Mr. Reynolds was writing something in his red notebook. When they came out on to the landing, Mr. Eliot stopped to admire the oak linen chest in which the blankets were kept.

'What a beautiful chest,' he said.

'It belonged to my mother,' said Aunt Em graciously. 'It was given to her by the lady—a titled lady—she was maid to. You'll see that it's carved on the inside of the lid as well,' she added, thinking, as she opened the chest, how snowy white her blankets looked.

'Admirable,' said Mr. Eliot, running his fingers over the carving.

Aunt Em stood smiling until she suddenly remembered that her secret post office savings book lay at the bottom of the chest under the blankets. She moved forward and pulled down the lid so quickly that Mr. Eliot almost trapped his fingers. He seemed rather startled by her abrupt movements.

123

'Perhaps you would like a cup of tea, sir?' said Aunt Em, thinking of the best tea service all newly washed and ready, and the fruit cake, now three days old, but none the worse for that.

Mr. Eliot glanced at Mr. Mason.

'Well, there are other lodge houses to see, Mr. Eliot,' he said. 'I really think that we should be going.'

Mr. Reynolds again wrote something in his notebook, and the visit was over.

'Thank you, Mrs. Potter,' said Mr. Eliot as Aunt Em stood by the front door and watched her visitors leave. 'You have been most helpful.'

Aunt Em's curtsy did not include Mr. Reynolds. She would have liked to have seen what was written in his red notebook.

'Did the company call, then?' said Uncle Percy when he came home in the evening.

'Yes,' replied Aunt Em. 'That Mr. Eliot seemed well enough— for a Londoner.'

Uncle Percy did not ask why a large fruit cake should appear on the table for an ordinary week-day tea.

The next morning Mr. Mason went with Mr. Eliot and Mr. Reynolds to Penrose Farm. They spent a long time talking with the Master in the dining-room and then Miss Nell showed them the house. They came into the kitchen and stood for a moment watching Kate as she made an apple pie. She hated being watched as she worked, but Miss Nell gave her an encouraging smile. Mr. Eliot wished her good morning, and then they went into the dairy.

Kate thought that he seemed a very pleasant gentleman. After chapel last Sunday people had stayed to talk about Mr. Eliot's impending visit, and the feeling was that perhaps he would give them notice to leave their cottages.

'I've been at Rose Cottage nigh on forty-five years,' said Mr. Willett. 'I don't want to be looking for another house at my time of life.'

'Still, I don't suppose for one moment that he'd bring a great load of London folks down here to live,' said Mrs. Hives comfortingly. 'They wouldn't know what to do with themselves, just the same as we wouldn't know what to do up in London.'

After Mr. Eliot had been shown the farmhouse, he went to inspect the farm buildings. The men in the yard touched their caps and went about their work, aware of his watchful eyes and the red notebook of Mr. Reynolds.

'You've been farming here for nearly thirty years, I believe, Mr. Linden?' Mr. Eliot said.

'Yes,' replied the Master. 'My tenancy agreement was first of all drawn up with Sir Charles in 1885. When he died, his son, Sir Edward, let the agreement continue on the same terms.'

'I see,' said Mr. Eliot. 'Well, I must say that I've been very impressed with all that I've seen. Thank you for your time and trouble. Good day to you.'

The next week was an anxious time for nearly everyone living in Bretherton as they wondered what the outcome of Mr. Eliot's visit would be. Almost all the houses and cottages belonged to the Ellswood Park estate. The cottage where the Bassetts lived was one of the very few exceptions. Mr. Blake, for whom Mr. Bassett worked, owned his own farm and three cottages as well.

'It's all right for you. You've got nothing to worry about,' said Aunt Em, conveniently forgetting that she had once suggested that the Bassetts should move down into the village. 'I dare say that there are quite a few people shaking in their boots.'

Then the news came that Mr. Eliot had bought the estate. Although Lady Margaret would be leaving the village immediately, everything would continue in the same way. Mr. Linden's tenancy agreement would continue under the same terms with Mr. Eliot and the entire staff at Ellswood Park was to remain.

'Which is no more than what was really expected,' Aunt Em said, 'though if it had been me that had anything to do with it, there's some as would have been weeded out.'

She had discovered that after Mr. Eliot had left her house on the afternoon of the inspection, he had gone on to North Lodge where he had taken tea with the fourth gamekeeper's wife, Mrs. Croucher.

'And I suppose she's crowing over everybody about that,' she said, when Uncle Percy told her what had happened. 'All I can say is that this Mr. Eliot can't be used to very much if he can sit down and drink a cup of tea up at North Lodge with that Mrs. Croucher. She's never got her apron off from morning till night, and her washing is an absolute disgrace. If it was me, I'd be ashamed to put such sheets and blankets out on the clothes-line.

You can always tell what sort of a housekeeper a woman is by the colour of her washing.'

Aunt Em always liked to be first with any news. She was able to tell Mrs. Bassett that Mr. Eliot had a wife and three sons and owned a large munitions factory in London.

'He's probably making a tidy pile out of the war,' she said. 'Well, it stands to reason that he must be. I expect that Lady Margaret is a hard woman to do business with.'

'What did you think of Mr. Eliot?' asked Mrs. Bassett.

'Well enough,' replied Aunt Em. 'Not what I call proper gentry, mind you, and he never will be, not even if he lived to be a hundred. But there's one thing I will say, though,' she added generously, 'there's no denying that he knows a good piece of furniture when he sees it.'

Chapter 13

After the anxiety felt in the village concerning the future of the Ellswood Park estate ended with the announcement that Mr. Eliot was the new owner, life for the inhabitants of Bretherton continued as before.

Aunt Em had been the first person to see the new mistress of Ellswood Park. When she opened the lodge gates to her pony and trap, Mrs. Eliot had nodded graciously from under a cream-coloured parasol and Aunt Em had dutifully curtsied.

'Quite a fine-looking woman,' she admitted to Mrs. Bassett. 'Not like Lady Margaret, of course, but well enough.'

Mr. Eliot remained in London from Tuesday until Friday, and then was met at Chaxton railway station by a groom from the Park. Often he was accompanied by week-end guests.

'Usually about eight or nine ladies and gentlemen,' said Aunt Em, 'with so much luggage that you'd think they were staying for a month at least, instead of going back to London on Monday afternoon. I dare say it's a fine enough world for some people.'

Dinner was always on the table at South Lodge at twelve o'clock, and Aunt Em felt particularly annoyed when she had to leave her meal and go and open the lodge gates for the Eliots and their guests when they drove back from morning service every Sunday. When Lady Margaret had lived at Ellswood Park she had always gone for a short drive before returning for luncheon at one o'clock.

'She used to arrive at the lodge gates regularly as a clock at quarter to one,' said Aunt Em. 'And it meant that a body could at least have her own dinner in peace.'

Kate wrote to Liza Hibberd telling her of all the changes that had taken place, and in the letter which Liza wrote in reply, she told Kate that her two brothers had left the barracks at Aldershot and were now in France.

In the hedges, the blackthorn blossom which Kate always thought was one of the loveliest of flowers, gave way to the thickly clustering may and the fields were bright with the gleam of buttercups. Then, with the fine weather in June, it was time for haymaking and the Master and the men often worked in the fields until nine o'clock in the evening. The stone jars in wicker baskets were again carried down from the attic next to Kate's bedroom and she and Miss Nell drove down to the fields with beer for the men. Sometimes when she saw the sadness in Miss Nell's face, Kate longed to say something to try and comfort her, but Sir Edward's name was never mentioned at Penrose Farm.

One afternoon Miss Nell was showing Kate how to skin a rabbit, when suddenly there was a loud knocking on the back door. When Kate opened it, she found Bert Dixon standing there. His face was very red and he was breathing heavily as if he had been running.

'Is Miss Nell there, maid?' he said.

Kate turned to go back, but Miss Nell was already behind her, saying in an unusually sharp voice, 'Yes, Bert. What is it?'

'It's the Master, miss,' said Bert. 'He seems to have been taken bad, all of a sudden. We thought it best not to move him. The lad has gone across the fields for the doctor.'

Miss Nell ran down the garden path and Bert followed more slowly behind her. Kate went back into the kitchen and put the skinned rabbit into a bowl of water, thinking of the serious expression on Bert Dixon's face, and the speed with which Miss Nell had run down the path. The house seemed very still and she sat in a chair with her arms folded in her lap, as if waiting for something. Then she heard the sound of a pony and trap and she ran out to the side gate and saw that it was the doctor, with Tom Collier sitting beside him. Tom looked very hot and flushed, and Kate realized that he must have run through six fields to reach the doctor's house.

'Out you get, lad,' said the doctor. 'Go inside and rest for a few minutes.'

Tom followed Kate into the kitchen and sat in her armchair, while she filled a glass with water.

'Thanks, Kate,' Tom said as he took the glass. After drinking the water, he lay back in the armchair with his eyes closed. The long-case clock in the hall struck three, and Kate remembered that the Master always wound it up each Saturday night.

'Would you like some more water, Tom?' she asked.

'Reckon I would,' said Tom. Kate was glad when he sat up. He had looked so hot and weary lying back in the chair.

'We were in the bottom meadow,' he said. 'The Master wanted to clear the hay from there by tonight. He was working with Jack Bray when suddenly he fell down in the hay, almost as if he had a stroke or something. Jack started to unbutton his collar and then Bert Dixon came running up and told me to fetch the doctor as fast as I could. I went through the fields because I thought it would be the quickest way. I had to run all through the long grass. When I got to the doctor's house, the maid said he was already out on a call. She said I could wait, but I thought I'd better not, and just as I was coming down the drive, the doctor was coming along the main road, and he told me to jump up in the trap and we drove straight here.'

They sat in silence in the kitchen, and at half past three Kate began to set out the cups and saucers, and filled the kettle from the pump and put it on the range, glad of something to do. She went out into the garden to fetch the two tea towels she had hung out to dry after the dinner things had been washed up, and just as she was reaching up to take the pegs from the clothes-line, the gate in the back garden wall opened, and Miss Nell came in with the doctor, followed by some of the farm men.

'Go back into the kitchen and shut the door,' said the doctor, and Kate hurried inside.

'They've just come back,' she said to Tom, and they heard the heavy footsteps of the men and Bert Dixon's voice saying, 'Easy now,' as they went upstairs. Soon afterwards Bert Dixon came into the kitchen with his cap in his hand, and as she looked at him, Kate realized that it was the first time that she had seen him when he was not wearing the old tweed cap with the torn peak.

'I've got some bad news for you,' said Bert. 'We've just brought the Master home. He's dead.'

Please let him be wrong, thought Kate. Miss Nell has had too much sadness.

'I ran as fast as I could for the doctor,' said Tom.

'I know you did, lad,' said Bert, 'and there's no one to say anything different. It was a heart attack. No one could have done anything for him.' He turned to Kate. 'Miss Nell's upstairs, maid. Jack Bray's gone to fetch his wife. She'll be here in a few minutes. Stay here, young Tom, with Kate until Mrs. Bray gets here.'

He went out of the kitchen and Kate and Tom stood looking at one another.

'Oh, Tom,' said Kate, and he came and put his arm round her.

'We were going to have roast rabbit tomorrow,' said Kate sadly.

She thought of the first time that she had seen the Master. She had stood awkwardly in the kitchen, not knowing what to do when she saw him sitting at the kitchen table, and he had looked across at her and smiled, and told her not to work too hard on her first day.

Mrs. Bray came soon afterwards. 'This is a sad day's work and no mistake,' she said, and went upstairs.

'I'd best get back to work,' said Tom slowly. 'Thanks for the drink, Kate.'

Kate managed to smile at him as he went off. The kettle boiled over and the spluttering of the water on the range made her jump. It seemed a long time before Miss Nell and Mrs. Bray came back into the kitchen.

'We'll have that cup of tea now, Kate,' said Mrs. Bray, and Kate hurried to fill the teapot.

'There's nothing like a cup of tea, Miss Nell,' said Mrs. Bray.

Kate glanced at Miss Nell. Outwardly she seemed quite calm, but she was very pale. They sat for a while sipping their tea, and then Miss Nell said, 'Well, there's a lot to do. We must get on, I suppose.'

'Work's the best thing,' said Mrs. Bray.

After she had gone home, Kate and Miss Nell pulled down the blinds in all the rooms and then they went out into the garden and picked some sprays of the white rambler rose which grew against the front of the house. As she looked up at the windows, Kate thought how strange the house looked with all the blinds down. It was as if no one at all was living there. Miss Nell arranged the roses in the silver rose-bowl from the drawing-room and carried them upstairs.

After the tea things had been cleared away, Kate was usually able to have some time to herself until half past seven when she would begin to get the supper ready. Very often she read one of Miss Nell's books and wrote up the day's events in her diary. That evening, however, she was particularly busy receiving the people who came to the farm. A message had been sent to Ringstone

Farm and Miss Grace and Mr. Hurford arrived soon after six o'clock. The undertaker came from the village and after he had driven away, the vicar came and Kate showed him into the drawing-room where Miss Nell sat talking with Miss Grace and Mr. Hurford. Mrs. Hives, the village dressmaker, came to the back door and went upstairs with Miss Nell and Miss Grace to discuss the clothes they would require for the funeral. Afterwards she came out into the kitchen and had a cup of tea.

'Well, this is a sad business, Kate,' she said, while they waited for the kettle to boil. 'Still, he couldn't have suffered any pain. Not like some poor souls that lay and linger for many a year. My man died suddenly. He came home from a day's work, had his tea, and just sat down in his chair and was gone. Twelve years now since he was taken.'

She was still wearing her tape measure round her neck. 'Now it's to be dresses for Miss Nell and Miss Grace, and a coat and a skirt for you.'

Kate had not thought about any mourning clothes. Mrs. Hives saw the surprised look on her face.

'I'm only following Miss Nell's instructions, Kate,' she explained. 'You count as family. She said that you were to have a black costume for walking out on Sundays.'

After Mrs. Hives had taken Kate's measurements and had written them down in a little notebook, she had her cup of tea.

'That was Miss Grace's husband I saw out in the garden when I came in, I expect,' she said. 'Fine, well-set-up chap. You make a good cup of tea, Kate, not like some, all milk and hot water.' She looked at the clock. 'Is that the time? Well, this won't do, it's a tidy step back to the village. I told Miss Nell not to start worrying that the dresses won't be finished in time. They'll be up here on Friday, just as I promised. It wouldn't be the first time I've sat up all night at my sewing machine to get something finished. Your costume will take a bit longer, but you shall have it just as soon as I get it done.'

The next morning Kate carried only one brass can of hot water upstairs at twenty past six for Miss Nell and tiptoed past the closed door of the Master's room. She was preparing the breakfast tray when Miss Nell came into the kitchen.

'I'll have breakfast with you in here, Kate,' she said. She took the moustache cup with a peacock painted on it which the Master always used from the dresser and put it away in the china cabinet in the drawing-room.

It had been arranged that the Master was to be buried on Saturday afternoon, and Miss Grace came on Friday morning at ten o'clock. After dinner she and Miss Nell baked a batch of cakes and scones, while Kate washed all the extra cups and saucers and plates which would be needed for the funeral tea, thinking as she did so that the last time the best tea service had been brought out was when Miss Grace and Mr. Hurford were married. Miss Nell and Miss Grace made small attempts at cheering each other up, which Kate thought made the occasion even more sad.

On the morning of the funeral Mrs. Bray and Mrs. Crewe came to the farmhouse to prepare for the funeral tea, and from one o'clock onwards relatives and the many people who had liked and respected the Master began to arrive. At quarter to two the coffin was carried out of the house by six of the farm men, and Miss Nell, walking with the Master's brother, and Miss Grace with Mr. Hurford following, led the long line of mourners to the waiting carriages and pony traps. Kate stood in the hall with Mrs. Bray and Mrs. Crewe and to her it seemed so strange that the sun could shine so brightly, almost as if it mocked the sadness of the day.

'Well, we shan't see his like again,' said Mrs. Bray heavily.

'No, indeed,' said Mrs. Crewe.

They went back into the kitchen and began to carry the trays with the cups and saucers and plates into the dining-room and the drawing-room. Miss Nell was to pour out the tea in the drawing-room with Kate helping her, and Miss Grace and Mrs. Bray were to be in the dining-room, while Mrs. Crewe was to stay in the kitchen keeping the kettles on the boil, seeing that the farm men had their tea, and making any more sandwiches that would be required.

'I'm downright glad that Miss Nell arranged it like that,' she said to Kate. 'I never feel comfortable mixing in with the gentry. I'm all right in the kitchen, but I was never cut out to be a parlour-maid.'

Everything was ready when the mourners came back from the funeral service. Kate stood beside Miss Nell as she poured the tea and handed the cups round to the visitors, most of whom she recognized as having been guests at Miss Grace's wedding. Then the women had worn pretty, pastel dresses. Today they were in sombre black. When Kate had served everyone she went out into the kitchen for some more scones. Mrs. Crewe was pouring out tea for the farm men, all of whom wore black armbands.

'Back again already, Kate?' said Mrs. Crewe. 'It seems as if there's nothing like a funeral to give folks a good appetite.'

When Kate went out into the passage with her tray, she followed her out-

side and said, 'How's that Miss Nell? Is she bearing up all right?'

'Yes, she's all right,' said Kate, but when she went back with her tray she watched Miss Nell as she moved round the drawing-room speaking to everyone. It seemed to her that it was only when people said something especially kind to Miss Nell that her self-control faltered. It seemed strange to see her wearing a black dress. It made her look so pale and ill.

Miss Grace and Mr. Hurford and the guests from the dining-room came in to hear the Master's will read. There was silence in the room when Mr. Powell, the lawyer from Chaxton, cleared his throat and stood up. The will was quite short. It had been drawn up a fortnight after the Master's wife had died. Everything he possessed was to be divided equally between Miss Nell and Miss Grace.

'That was no more than what we expected,' an old man whispered to his wife, and she nodded in agreement.

Afterwards Miss Nell, Miss Grace, and Mr. Hurford stood in the hall and shook hands with all the people as they left, and then they sat in the garden talking, while Kate, Mrs. Bray, and Mrs. Crewe cleared everything away. In the evening Kate and Miss Nell sat quietly in the kitchen. The house seemed very empty after everyone had gone.

Mrs. Hives brought Kate's new black costume on the following Thursday and also a white blouse and a wide-brimmed black hat to wear with it. Kate felt a little self conscious when she went home on Sunday afternoon, and May, who usually clamoured to sit on her lap, hung back and seemed rather overawed by the tall figure in black who seemed so strange and different from Kate in her brown dress. Mrs. Bassett admired the coat and skirt, but thought how touching it was to see Kate dressed in mourning clothes. Aunt Em felt the material and counted the buttons on the sleeves and pursed her lips knowingly.

'Well,' she said, 'there's no denying that the Lindens certainly know how to do things properly, and nobody can say anything different. I wouldn't be surprised if that material didn't cost a pretty penny.'

She glanced at Kate. 'I wonder what your Miss Nell will do now?' she said.

'I don't know,' said Kate quietly.

'Well, I don't suppose you would,' said Aunt Em. For the first time in her life she felt a sense of reproof in the quiet tones of her niece, and she tried to hide her anger by saying quickly, 'I can't see her telling everybody her business and having it gossiped about by all the village rag and bobtail. But it stands to reason that she'll have to do something. It's a big farm and it needs a lot of running. It's a pity that she's not married. It's a hard life for a woman on her own. Still, those that live longest will see the most.'

Chapter 14

Even if Aunt Em wondered what Miss Nell would do now that the Master was dead, only two immediate changes took place at Penrose Farm. Miss Nell no longer used the dining-room, but instead had all her meals in the kitchen with Kate, and Bert Dixon began to come up to the farmhouse every morning for the orders. The pattern of the work continued as it had done so when the Master was there. Kate realized that although she had lived in his house for more than a year, she had not really seen a great deal of Mr. Linden. She had been aware of his presence by the sound of his deep voice in the dining-room and the sound of his footsteps in the passage as he went out to the farmyard, and it was the silence in the house that she now noticed most of all.

One morning Mr. Powell, the lawyer, came to discuss the new tenancy agreement with Miss Nell.

'I've been in touch with Mr. Mason, the agent, but he says that Mr. Eliot is remaining in London for a week. Apparently there's an important contract to be settled for some work at his factory,' said Mr. Powell, 'so I thought that I would go through all the points of the agreement with you first of all, Miss Linden, and then I can negotiate with Mr. Eliot when he returns.'

'If possible I would like to continue here under exactly the same terms as my father had with Sir Edward Carey,' said Miss Nell, in a voice which trembled a little.

'Quite so,' said the lawyer. 'As I thought. There should be no difficulty there. It is quite possible of course that a higher rent may be asked, but I'm sure that both you and Mr. Eliot will be able to reach an agreed settlement.'

On Monday of the following week Miss Nell and Kate drove into Chaxton in order that Miss Nell could settle the details of the new farm tenancy. They left the pony and trap at the livery stables of the Rose and Crown and walked to the market-place.

People glanced sympathetically at the two black-clad figures as they passed.

'I don't know how long I shall be,' said Miss Nell, 'but have a leisurely look round all the market stalls, and then meet me outside the Corn Exchange at half past three.'

First of all Kate went to the post office to put five shillings in her banking account. Her savings had been steadily growing. The man who usually sat at the savings bank counter was not there, and instead, Kate was attended to by a young woman.

As she checked the entry in her book, a man asked, 'Where's the young man, then?' and the woman said that he had enlisted.

'They reckoned that the war would be over by Christmas,' said the man. 'They didn't say which one though.'

In the market there were the usual number of stalls. Kate bought two reels of cotton and then she walked slowly round looking at everything. She stopped at a second-hand stall where all the goods displayed had come from people's homes, either because they had died, or because they had sold up and gone to live with a son or daughter. To Kate it seemed rather sad to see ornaments and pots and pans, parts of tea services, candlesticks, oil lamps, and boxes of cutlery piled in untidy heaps. Everything looked so forlorn. Aunt Em came to the market every week and she always made a point of visiting the second-hand stalls. She prided herself on always being able to find bargains, and would spend quite a long time handling everything, her sharp eyes looking for any cracks or chips in the goods displayed. In the parlour of South Lodge which no one ever entered except Aunt Em, there was a whatnot whose shelves were filled with all the bargains she had found at the market.

'It's surprising what you can find there,' she said. 'Of course, you have to have your wits about you and your eyes open. I always make them bring the price down before I say I'll buy anything.'

Aunt Em did not realize that the stallholders soon began to recognize her as she made her weekly visits, and consequently they said that an article was dearer than it really was, so that Aunt Em could make them lower the price thinking that she had one of her bargains.

Suddenly a voice said, 'It's Kate, isn't it?' and when Kate turned from the stall, she saw that it was Nancy, the girl who had met her outside the school the day that she had come to Chaxton to take the Labour Examination. Although her auburn hair was hidden under a straw hat, she still had the same cheerful grin. She looked at Kate's black costume with sympathetic eyes.

'Are you in mourning?' she asked gently.

Kate told her about the Master.

'At first I thought that perhaps you had lost somebody in the war,' said Nancy. 'My brother enlisted last May. He's somewhere in France—though no one really knows where. My mother starts worrying if there isn't a letter from him each week.'

Kate remembered how Miss Nell always looked forward to letters from Sir Edward, and she herself had always felt glad when she saw the postman coming up the garden path every Thursday.

'Where are you working?' she asked.

'I had to go into service after all,' said Nancy with a rueful smile. 'There weren't any vacancies at Billington's. I'm kitchen-maid at St. John's vicarage.'

'Do you like it?' said Kate.

'Well, it's all right, I suppose,' replied Nancy. 'When I get a bit older I shall probably look for another place. The cook has got a bit of a temper, and on some days nothing that I do ever seems to please her. Sometimes I think I'm back at school again. We have prayers in the hall every morning, and sometimes I haven't got a clean apron to put on, and then the mistress starts staring over the top of her spectacles with a face like the back of a thundercloud.'

They both laughed. 'Is this your half day?' said Nancy.

'No,' said Kate. 'I just came in with Miss Nell.'

'You are lucky,' said Nancy. 'I never have any outings like that. I'm only out now because the mistress wanted to send a letter. There's a post box quite close to the vicarage, but she wanted it to go from the post office, so out I had to come. Not that I really mind. I thought that I'd walk through the market on the way back. All the same, I'd better be off, I suppose. I shouldn't be at all surprised if Cook didn't time me. Glad to have seen you. Perhaps I'll see you again.'

'Good-bye,' called Kate, as Nancy hurried off with a great nodding of the straw hat.

It was quarter past three when Kate walked slowly back to the Corn Exchange. Miss Nell was already there waiting for her.

'I was earlier than I thought,' said Miss Nell. 'The papers weren't ready for me to sign. Mr. Powell said that everything hadn't been settled with Mr. Eliot yet.'

As they walked back to the Rose and Crown, Miss Nell seemed rather thoughtful, and once they had left the main road and were driving in the lanes to Bretherton, she asked Kate to take the reins.

Two days later Mr. Powell came to the farm. Kate showed him into the dining-room and went out into the back garden to tell Miss Nell. She thought that he had probably brought the new tenancy agreement.

'I expect he would like a glass of wine,' said Miss Nell as she went indoors. 'The elderberry, I think.'

Kate took extra care as she prepared the tray, using one of the best lace-edged tray cloths and polishing the glasses until they gleamed like crystal. Everything was ready when Miss Nell rang. As she went into the dining-room Kate heard the lawyer say, 'and I would like you to know that I did everything I could to persuade Mr. Eliot to change his mind, but he was adamant. He's a very hard man to deal with, Miss Linden. It seems that Penrose Farm is far more productive than the home farm on the Ellswood Park estate.'

'It seems a poor return for all my father's hard work,' said Miss Nell quietly, as Kate placed the tray in front of her.

As she went along the passage she wondered what it was that the lawyer had said to Miss Nell. She looked so pale and worried. When Mr. Powell had driven away, Miss Nell came into the kitchen with the tray.

'Kate,' she said, 'I want you to go out and find Bert Dixon. Will you tell him that I want him to bring all the men up to the house at five o'clock?'

'Yes, Miss Nell,' said Kate, and she went down the garden path, crossed the small field, and walked into the farmyard. She was glad that the grey geese were nowhere in sight. Bert Dixon was just coming out of one of the cowsheds.

'Anything wrong, maid?' he called.

When Kate gave him the message, he looked grave. 'Tell Miss Nell five o'clock it shall be, then,' he said.

'It's bad news, I'm afraid,' Miss Nell said to Kate when she came back. 'Mr. Powell came to tell me that I'm not going to be able to stay on here at Penrose Farm.'

'What will you do, Miss Nell?' asked Kate.

'I just don't know,' she said with a sad smile. 'Everything seems to be changing so quickly. It seems that nothing lasts.' She went to the dresser and took down the pewter inkstand. 'Now I must write a letter to Miss Grace, and then perhaps you'd take it down to the post box.'

As she waited for the letter to be written, Kate remembered what Aunt Em had said when the Master died. 'It's a hard life for a woman on her own. Still, those that live longest will see the most.' She could not imagine being at Penrose Farm without Miss Nell.

At five o'clock all the men came to the back door, and Miss Nell went out to speak to them with Kate standing behind her. There were serious looks on the men's faces.

'I have asked you to come here so that you will all know what is happening,' said Miss Nell. 'This morning Mr. Powell came to tell me that Mr. Eliot will not grant me a new tenancy agreement so that I can continue here at Penrose Farm. When my father died the agreement which he had with Mr. Eliot naturally ended. Mr. Eliot is quite within his rights to refuse to accept me as the new tenant. I have to leave by Michaelmas at the latest, earlier if at all possible.'

Standing behind Miss Nell, Kate could see her clenching and unclenching her hands in her efforts to speak calmly and steadily. She was aware of the stillness of the men.

'Who'll be the new tenant, Miss Nell?' said Bert Dixon.

'Mr. Eliot will put his own bailiff here,' said Miss Nell.

The men stared uneasily at each other, twisting their caps in their hands.

'Regarding your jobs,' said Miss Nell resolutely, 'I don't know how many men Mr. Eliot and his bailiff will need. The bailiff will be coming on Friday and we shall know more then. This is all I can tell you at the moment. You know as much as I do.'

Bert Dixon cleared his throat.

'Well, Miss Nell,' he said, 'this has come as a shock and no mistake. I know I speak for us all when I say that we're downright sorry to hear what you've had to say. And it's not only ourselves we're thinking about. I've been here twenty years and I've always been treated fair and proper by the Master and by you. I'm right sorry that it should come to this.'

'Thank you, Bert,' said Miss Nell. She stood and watched the men go silently down the garden path, each busy with his own thoughts. She knew that there would be anxious wives in the cottages that night. Her eyes were very bright as she went back into the kitchen.

'It looks as if we shall have to find you a new situation, Kate,' she said. 'I can only say to you what I've just said to the men. It's a question of what the new people will want. The bailiff's wife may need someone to help her in the house, or she may bring someone with her.'

'I don't think that I would want to stay on here working for someone else,' said Kate.

'We'll see,' said Miss Nell. 'There will be no need to decide anything yet. I shan't have to leave here until September.'

On Friday Mr. Pritchard, the bailiff, and his wife drove to Penrose Farm. Mr. Pritchard went with Bert Dixon to see the farm buildings, and his wife was shown over the house by Miss Nell.

Kate was preparing the afternoon tea when they came into the kitchen.

'This is Kate,' said Miss Nell.

Kate curtsied and said good afternoon.

'Good afternoon,' said Mrs. Pritchard. She was a tall, grey-haired woman with deep-set eyes and a pursed mouth.

'You trust her with the tea caddy, then,' she said to Miss Nell, as Kate measured the tea into the pot.

'Certainly,' said Miss Nell.

'She's a big girl,' said Mrs. Pritchard, speaking as if Kate was unable to hear what she said.

She began to look at the kitchen fittings, at the kitchen range, and the pump by the sink. She ran her fingers along one of the dresser shelves and seemed quite disappointed that there was no dust mark on the whiteness of her glove. She watched as Kate took the cake from the cake tin and began to butter slices of bread.

'You're main heavy-handed with the butter, aren't you, miss?' said Mrs. Pritchard. 'It's easy to see that you don't have to pay for your keep.'

Miss Nell picked up the tray. 'If you'd like to go back into the dining-room, Mrs. Pritchard,' she said firmly, 'we can have our tea in there.'

Alone in the kitchen Kate found that she was trembling as she poured her own tea. The calculated rudeness of Mrs. Pritchard had upset her, and she thought that in an underhand way she had also criticized Miss Nell. She thought how sad it must have been for Miss Nell to have had to show the bailiff's wife over the house, with Mrs. Pritchard looking at everything with such sharp, inquisitive eyes.

Miss Nell came back into the kitchen.

'Mrs. Pritchard would like to have a word with you, Kate,' she said. 'She's going to ask you if you would like to stay on here and work for her.'

'I think that it would be better if I looked for something else,' said Kate.

'I think so too,' said Miss Nell. 'Still, go into the dining-room and listen to what she has to say.'

Mrs. Pritchard was just pouring herself another cup of tea when Kate went into the dining-room. All the bread and butter had disappeared and there was only one slice of cake left. Mrs. Pritchard did not ask her to sit down.

'Well now, young woman,' she said, 'I dare say you've had your ears and eyes open and you know how things are. Miss Linden will have to be gone from here by Michaelmas and Mr. Pritchard will be coming to take over the farm. I've been told that you are a good worker, but I prefer to make my own judgements. However, I'm ready to give you a month's trial to see if you suit me.'

'No, thank you,' said Kate.

'Why not?' said Mrs. Pritchard in surprise. 'Have you got yourself fixed up already, then? If you have, you've been quick off the mark, I must say.'

'No,' said Kate firmly. 'I'll stay until Miss Nell goes, and then I'll look for another situation.'

'Well, I suppose that you know your own business best,' said Mrs. Pritchard, 'but if you're like most girls of your age, I very much doubt it. Jobs aren't all that easy to get, you know. Still, if you want to pass up this chance I'm offering you, there's nothing more to be said.'

'May I take the tray?' said Kate.

'Yes,' said Mrs. Pritchard carelessly.

It was a small triumph for Kate to be able to put the cake plate with the one slice of cake back on the tray. Mrs. Pritchard watched her closely as she went out of the room. She was annoyed that Kate was not going to stay. Such a big, strong girl too, she thought, but with an appetite to match, I shouldn't wonder.

Miss Nell looked questioningly at Kate when she went back into the kitchen.

'It's all right,' said Kate. 'I just told her that I wouldn't be staying after you had left. I managed to rescue one piece of cake,' she said, indicating the plate. She began to laugh and eventually Miss Nell joined in, their laughter helping to dispel Mrs. Pritchard's rudeness.

'I couldn't get that girl of yours to stay on,' said Mrs. Pritchard when Miss Nell went into the dining-room. 'Still, I dare say that it will be her loss, not mine.'

'I thought that perhaps you would be bringing a maid of your own,' said Miss Nell.

'I thought that I'd make a fresh start,' said Mrs. Pritchard. She did not tell Miss Nell that she had never before been able to afford to have help in the house, and the bailiff's position which Mr. Eliot had offered to her husband would mean a considerable increase in their standard of living, but from her rude behaviour in the kitchen, Miss Nell thought that she had never before employed a maid. She was saddened by the thought that Mrs. Pritchard would be the new mistress of Penrose Farm, and was glad that Kate was not going to stay, in spite of the uncertainty of finding a new position. It was with a sense of relief that she watched the Pritchards drive away.

'Tell your mother what has happened, Kate,' said Miss Nell, 'and what you have decided, and then the next time we go into Chaxton we can call at Miss Maxwell's agency and see what vacancies she has on her books.'

'I'd like to stay until September,' said Kate, 'or for as long as you need anyone.'

'You're more than just anyone,' said Miss Nell.

'What did you think of the bailiff, then?' asked Bert Dixon's wife, when he went home for tea.

'Not much,' said Bert grimly. 'He was poking his fingers into everything. It seems as if he isn't going to trust anybody. Some difference between him and the Master.' He sighed and stared at the bottom of his teacup. 'I reckon things are going to be very different up at the farm, lass. Still, we must be grateful for a job and a roof over our heads, I suppose.'

When Kate went home on the following Sunday she found that Mr. and Mrs. Bassett had already heard that Mr. Eliot would not allow Miss Nell to stay at Penrose Farm. Everyone in the village had been surprised by the action he had taken and they all sympathized with Miss Nell. Kate told her parents that she wanted to stay until Miss Nell left the farm and when she told them about Mrs. Pritchard, they agreed that it would be best for her to try to find an entirely new position.

'You'll find that there's a world of difference in people,' said Mrs. Bassett.

Aunt Em arrived soon afterwards and settled herself comfortably in the parlour.

'Well, I suppose you'll soon be packing your trunk,' she said to Kate.

'Not until Miss Nell goes,' said Kate, wishing that Aunt Em would not ask so many questions about matters which did not really concern her.

'Well, you've no call to wait until Michaelmas,' said Aunt Em in surprise. 'You want to go into the agency at Chaxton and get yourself fixed up with another place just as soon as you can. It's no good hanging on there until that Miss Nell leaves and then finding yourself with no place to go to.' She glanced at Mrs. Bassett. 'Of course,' she said, 'if I'd been allowed to speak for you at Ellswood Park when you left school, you'd have been settled in there very comfortably now, with nothing to worry about, instead of having to go traipsing round looking for work.'

'I've had a good place at Penrose Farm,' said Kate. 'I've been happy there and Miss Nell has always been very good to me. I'm glad that I didn't go to Ellswood Park, and from the way Mr. Eliot has treated Miss Nell, I don't think that he would be worth working for, anyway.'

'Hoity toity,' said Aunt Em, but she admitted to herself that Kate was right. Mr. Eliot wasn't what she would call real gentry. She'd thought that from the very moment she had set eyes on him.

Chapter 15

Mr. Hurford and Miss Grace had asked Miss Nell to make her home with them, but she had gently refused their offer. She was to leave Penrose Farm after the corn had been harvested and then she was going to Derbyshire to be housekeeper to her uncle.

It seemed to Kate that the last few weeks passed very quickly. Each Sunday evening as she walked back to the farmhouse after her half day, she looked at the corn in the fields on each side of the lane and realized that it would soon be harvest-time.

'I reckon we can start cutting on Friday,' said Bert Dixon one morning, when he came into the kitchen for his orders. There was a feeling of sadness as the reaping began. As she stood watching the men at work, Kate thought that the second harvest was even more bountiful than that of the previous year. It was almost as if the land was determined to give of its best for Miss Nell. Kate remembered that the gipsy woman had said that between the two harvests there would be a great many changes. No one had ever dreamed of the events which would cause them to be made. She was not really sure that she believed that anyone could foretell the future, but when she thought of what the gipsy had told her, of how she would one day meet someone in a large town who would be very dear to her, she wondered if it would really happen.

She remembered her first harvest at the farm, and the harvest-home supper which the Master had given for all the farm men and their wives. Mrs. Bray and Mrs. Crewe were guests at this celebration and so Miss Grace had come to help Miss Nell and Kate. Two long tables were set out end to end to make one long table on the front lawn. There had been a fine supper of cold roast beef, mashed potatoes, and salad, with chutney and pickles. Afterwards there was apple pie and cream. The guests began to arrive at seven o'clock and at first they had stood rather awkwardly by the front gate, but the Master was there to welcome them and Miss Grace and Miss Nell came out to take the wives indoors and to show them where to hang up their hats and coats. Then they all sat down at the long table with their husbands, while Miss Nell, Miss Grace, and Kate hurried round seeing that everyone had plenty to eat, and the Master and Mr. Hurford carried round great stoneware jugs of beer and cider. There was dandelion wine for the wives.

'Lovely drop of wine,' Mrs. Bray had said to Miss Nell, and Kate wondered if Miss Nell remembered the day on which the dandelions had been picked. After the meal was over, the Master had proposed a toast to the prosperity of the farm, and then Bert Dixon had stood up and said solemnly, 'I ask you all to drink a toast to the Master,' and everyone had stood facing Mr. Linden, each with a mug or a glass in his hand, while he sat smiling and looking round at them all.

'And a toast to Miss Nell and Miss Grace,' said Bert, and at that Miss Grace and Miss Nell smiled and nodded their thanks. The Master handed out tobacco to the men, and Miss Nell and Miss Grace sat talking quietly to the women, asking about the children and the older girls away in service, while Mr. Crewe took a tin whistle from his pocket and began to play all the old country tunes which he played when he stayed up all night in his wooden hut when it was lambing time. It had been a very happy occasion with the feeling of contentment which comes from the realization of the successful ending of a long and important task. As Kate had sat looking round the long table it seemed difficult to think of the country being at war. She thought of the harvest hymns and the lines 'All is safely gathered in, Ere the winter storms begin', and then she had suddenly become aware of Tom Collier watching her from over the rim of his mug of cider.

This year, when all the harvesting was ended, because of her period of mourning, Miss Nell did not give a harvest supper. Instead the men received an extra week's wages on the last Saturday, and as she paid each man, Miss Nell thanked him and shook him by the hand.

Most of the farmhouse furniture and all the farm stock and implements were to be sold. Miss Grace came to choose the things which she would take back to Ringstone Farm.

'There's so much that I'd like to keep,' she said to Miss Nell. 'It seems so hard to think of everything having to go among strangers.'

146

They made a list of the pieces of furniture which they did not wish to be sold and one of the big waggons was used to take them back to Ringstone Farm. Bert Dixon and Fred Chivers were there to load the furniture and Kate watched as the long-case clock from the hall was carried out, the Master's bureau which had stood in the dining-room and the marble-topped hall table, as well as sheets, pillow-cases, china, and glassware.

Miss Nell called Kate into the drawing-room.

'The auctioneer will be coming tomorrow to make a list of everything for the sale,' she said. 'Before he does that I would like you to have something from the china cabinet as a small keepsake of your time here. Choose anything you wish, Kate.'

As she looked at the china cabinet Kate thought of the times when she had helped Miss Nell to wash all the ornaments. They were so delicate and fragile that the big mixing bowl in which they were washed was lined with a piece of old flannel to prevent them from being cracked or chipped. She was always glad when the washing was ended and they were safely back on the shelves of the cabinet. She looked at the coffee cups and saucers, the dessert plates, and the collection of figurines, and she decided to choose a figure of a girl in a white kirtled dress, sprigged with grey and green, holding a bluebird in her hands.

'Thank you, Miss Nell,' Kate said, and Miss Nell just smiled and nodded. Kate wrapped the figurine in several sheets of tissue paper and placed it in her trunk.

The auctioneer came with two assistants to make the inventory. They walked all over the house looking at everything with a critical eye and Kate wondered how Miss Nell could appear to be so unmoved.

'That's a nice piece of furniture,' the auctioneer said, pointing to the dresser in the kitchen. 'That'll fetch a good price, Miss Linden.'

Kate glanced at Miss Nell and saw that the expression on her face was the same as when she had come back from the fields with the doctor on the afternoon that the Master had died.

Mr. Hurford bought Ladybird and the flock of sheep, and Mr. and Mrs. Crewe were moving to a cottage near Ringstone Farm. Bert Dixon and Tom Collier and the rest of the men were to stay and work for Mr. Pritchard.

The sale lasted for two days. All the farm implements were

set out in the small field behind the garden and a large crowd of people formed a ring round each item as it was offered for sale. Some of the big, grey carthorses were bought by the local farmers, but almost everything was purchased by Mr. Pritchard, acting on instructions from Mr. Eliot. The bailiff was already behaving as if he owned the farm, speaking in a loud voice to Mr. Jackson the auctioneer.

'It's easy to make a show with someone else's money,' muttered a man in the crowd. Kate wondered if the grey geese would dare to hiss at Mrs. Pritchard each time she went down to the farmyard.

On the morning of the second day of the sale, Kate took up Miss Nell's hot water with the sad thought that this was the last time that she would do so. The night before Miss Nell had paid her her wages and had given her extra money, enough to last for several weeks until she had found a new position. Miss Nell's trunks had already gone to Ringstone Farm where she was to stay for a few days before going on to Derbyshire to her uncle. Kate had finished packing her own trunk and it now stood in the hall. Miss Nell boiled two eggs for breakfast and Kate made some toast, but neither of them seemed to be very hungry. Afterwards they went upstairs and took the sheets, pillow-cases, and blankets from their beds and put them into a clothes basket to be sent to Mrs. Maslen, and soon after seven o'clock Mr. Jackson and four men arrived, and all the furniture was carried outside and placed on the lawn. All the pictures, china, cutlery, and glassware were arranged on three long trestle tables which the auctioneer had brought. Each item had a numbered ticket tied to it.

The sale was to begin at eleven o'clock, but people began to arrive quite early and walked among the furniture looking at everything, sitting in armchairs, feeling mattresses and cushions, and fingering the china and glassware. Miss Nell and Kate stood at the back of the crowd and watched as the auctioneer began to offer everything for sale. His small, deep-set eyes flashed among the crowd whenever a hand flickered or a nodding head indicated a bid. Aunt Em had come in search of bargains. When Kate saw her pushing her way through the crowd she hoped that she would not say anything which would embarrass Miss Nell, but fortunately she had just caught sight of Mrs. Maslen and she went to speak to her about the laundry.

'They've a good day for the sale,' said Aunt Em to Kate.

148

'And what a crowd here too. It's almost like a flower show. I see that there's several dealers from Chaxton here. I expect they've heard that there's some good stuff about.'

She took out her handkerchief and wiped her forehead. 'I didn't realize that it was such a long walk out here to the farm,' she went on. 'I must try and get a ride back in a cart if I can.'

She looked at Kate and saw the sadness in her face. Something touched her and she said in a gentle voice which no one had ever before heard her use, 'There now, Kate. Sometimes changes have to come and there's nothing that anyone can do to stop them.'

'Yes, I know,' said Kate with a sigh.

'Well now,' said Aunt Em, in her usual sharp voice. 'This won't do. There's a nice-looking decanter I've got my eye on— lot 203. I thought that it would be just right for the parlour— provided the price is right, of course. I'll see you before I go,' she said and she began to push her way through to the front of the crowd.

'Hello, Kate,' said a voice, and when Kate looked up Tom Collier was standing there.

'It doesn't seem right, somehow,' said Tom, 'people poking about, looking at everything.'

'No,' said Kate.

'Have you fixed up about a job?' asked Tom.

'I'm going into Chaxton in the morning,' said Kate, 'to see what there is at the agency. Miss Nell has written a reference for me.'

'Let me know how you get on,' said Tom.

'Yes, I will,' said Kate.

The sale ended at half past six and people began to drive away with their purchases in traps and carts. Aunt Em had bought the decanter and a set of blue jugs which used to stand on the top shelf of the pantry.

'I had to pay a bit more than I thought,' she admitted to Kate. 'Still, I'd made up my mind to have the decanter. And I'll get your uncle to pay for these jugs.'

She had also bought Kate's brown and yellow teapot.

'I bought this for next to nothing,' she said. 'No one else seemed to want it because it's a bit on the small side. I thought that you might like to have it, Kate, as a remembrance of your first place.'

Kate glanced at the teapot, remembering her first day at the farm when Miss Nell had taken it from the dresser cupboard. It seemed a long time ago.

'Don't you want it?' asked Aunt Em, wondering why Kate did not say anything.

'Oh yes, please, Aunt Em,' said Kate, hugging her.

'Careful,' said Aunt Em. 'What a strange girl you are. You nearly made me drop my basket.' She was pleased that her gift had brought so much pleasure to Kate. 'I can't stop because I'm having a ride back with Will Palmer and his wife. You can walk down to the gate with me and carry the basket.'

Outside in the lane Mr. and Mrs. Palmer were waiting with their horse and cart. Aunt Em scrambled up into the back of the cart and managed to find enough room to sit down among a brass bedstead, three chairs, a washstand, and a large jug and basin.

'See you on Sunday, then,' said Aunt Em as the cart moved off.

When all the people had gone, Kate walked back into the house. Now that the high-ceilinged rooms were empty they seemed very large. She thought of all the floors that she had scrubbed, all the paintwork she had washed, all the hot water that she had carried upstairs. Very soon she would be doing the same work again, but in another house, working for a new family. Tomorrow she would go to Miss Maxwell's agency in Chaxton and see what positions there were. She went upstairs to her own attic room, aware of the echoing sounds of her footsteps on the bare boards. She went to the uncurtained window and looked out, just as she had every morning at six o'clock to see what sort of a day it promised to be. She glanced down into the back garden and then looked across to the farm buildings. Bert Dixon was coming through the small field with Ladybird in the trap, so she went down to the hall where her hat and coat were lying on the top of the brown tin trunk. Miss Nell had just said good-bye to the auctioneer and was coming into the hall.

'Mr. Dixon's just bringing the trap, Miss Nell,' Kate said.

'All ready,' said Miss Nell with a little smile as she went upstairs.

Kate heard Bert Dixon's heavy boots in the passage.

'There you are, then, maid,' he said. 'Just the one trunk, is it?'

'Yes,' said Kate, following him through the scullery and into the side lane where Ladybird and the trap were waiting.

'I'll take the trap round to the front gate,' said Bert gruffly. 'Happen Miss Nell will lock the front door last of all.'

They drove round to the front of the house and waited for Miss Nell. Kate stared up at the warm, red bricks and the uncurtained windows, and after a little while Miss Nell came out and locked the front door and walked slowly down the garden path, a tall, slender figure in her long, black dress and big, black hat.

"There's the key, Bert,' she said with a smile which seemed to Kate to be far sadder than tears.

'Right, Miss Nell,' said Bert. 'Take care of yourself, maid, and you too, young Kate.'

He raised his hand in a kind of salute as Miss Nell and Kate drove away, and then he walked slowly home to his cottage.

As they drove past the fields Kate thought of the first time that she had come that way. The evening in the spring of the previous year she had walked rather forlornly by her father's side. Then the fields had been grey-green with the early corn and the leaves of the hedges had been slowly unfurling. Now as she rode in the trap beside Miss Nell, dressed in black, the leaves were already turning yellow, and in the fields there was only the pale stubble of the harvested corn. It seemed a long time ago that at school Miss Crompton had told her to write a composition about her favourite season. She had written about the autumn, and had described the many colours of the season, the tawny orange, the russet, yellow, and red of the woods and hedges. That evening she became aware of the underlying sadness of the autumn splendour. The crimson hawthorn berries and the orange rosehips in the hedges seemed to be not only bright splashes of colour, but also appeared as warnings of the hard winter that must follow.

When they reached the cottage, both Miss Nell and Kate climbed down from the trap and lifted down the brown tin trunk. Mrs. Bassett came to the parlour window and stood watching.

'This is good-bye, then, Kate,' said Miss Nell, taking her hand.

'Good-bye, Miss Nell,' Kate said, and she tried hard to make her voice as firm as Miss Nell's.

'Thank you for everything,' said Miss Nell.

That was all that she said, but Kate knew what she meant. She would never tell anyone—not even her mother and father—of Miss Nell's friendship with Sir Edward. It would always be a secret.

Miss Nell climbed back into the trap and drove slowly away. When she reached the curve in the lane, she turned and waved.

'Good-bye, Miss Nell,' said Kate softly, and she waved back until she could no longer see the trap. She stood looking down the lane, thinking of Sir Edward, and of how Miss Nell might have been Lady Ellen of Ellswood Park, with Aunt Em to open the lodge gates as she drove out in her carriage, but instead she was going to Derbyshire to be housekeeper to her uncle. She thought of Penrose Farm and of the Master, and of Mr. and Mrs. Pritchard, and she wondered how the men and Tom Collier would like working for them. Tomorrow she must go to the domestic agency at Chaxton and look for work.

Everything had changed. It seemed to her that she had come to the end of something in her life. She was not quite sure what it was, because she had thought that her childhood had ended when she went to the farm with the brown tin trunk which now stood in the road. She stood for a long time looking down the lane, and then she opened the white-painted gate and began to walk slowly down the garden path to the cottage. It was only then that Mrs. Bassett moved away from the window and came to the door to greet her.

'There now, Kate,' she said.